Save Me

Crysa James

ISBN 978-0-9989248-0-9

Printed in the United States of America

For Mom

To Linda, Janice, Nancy,
Patricia, and Carol.
I am so grateful for your candor, your
insight, and most of all, your friendship. You
inspire me to heights I never dreamed possible.

One

It was as dark inside as it was out. Closing the heavy door, he willed his eyes to adjust.

Quickly.

Mold and dust filled his nostrils. The shelter's interior, like its facade, had been built to withstand the ravages of time. Master craftsmanship etched every brick and log, right down to the stone and mortar fireplace.

The large room stretched to the back wall, creating a space only a giant would consider small. Overhead a loose weave of massive, rough-hewn wood beams supported the steeply pitched ceiling. Hand-planed boards lined every wall. Clay bricks paved an irregular floor. What few windows dotted the walls boasted glass panes, although locked shutters kept the outside completely out. The cavernous chamber shouted hard, severe angles. Only a homemade wooden table surrounded by three equally handcrafted chairs dissected the empty space.

Sounds of scampering stopped him dead in his tracks. Rats skittered in all directions.

With one exception.

Easily seven inches tall, squatting on its haunches, a lone rat stared directly at him. Even without benefit of light, he could see it, could see the beady black eyes, whiskers twitching as the rodent tested the air with its nose.

Most in his line of work would use this as an opportunity for target practice. Anyone who could draw a weapon, aim, and ultimately kill a wary, watching animal would have no problem utilizing the same maneuver on humans.

He, however, had no desire to take an innocent's life, whether human or animal. Even at the expense of target practice.

Especially---target practice.

He moved, knowing it would cause the animal to join its disappearing companions.

The animal's footfalls could be heard over his.

Long, smooth strides propelled him to a rack of serviceable shelves perched above one simple cabinet hugging the lower half of the far wall. Digging through paraphernalia left long ago, he was gratified to find a few candles. He fitted two tapers into crude candleholders but didn't light them.

He waited.

~*~

Lia Von Stratham halted her frantic pace the moment her destination came into view. Panting, she stared at the large stone cabin. Sweat trickled at her temples and down her back. Blinking rapidly, it was impossible to tell if the moisture in her eyes was from sweat or from tears of relief.

Shifting the heavy pack, containing every transportable medical supply available, temporarily eased the knots in her neck and back. She'd long ago ignored the pain of the straps cutting into her shoulders.

Absently she wiped away the sweat from her forehead with the sleeve of her Malken, the traditional neck-to-ankle gown native to this region. Temperatures in Southern Turkey climbed to uncomfortable heights in summer, even here in the mountains. At least the garment was cotton and breathed.

Moving toward the shepherd's home, Lia paid little attention to the deepening dusk. Waning rays of light transformed vivid hues of purples and pinks into sobering grays. Coming to a halt in front of the timeworn structure, Lia knocked loudly. After waiting for what seemed forever, she called out a tentative, "Hello?" Manners dictated she wait for an invitation even though it was doubtful a reply could be heard through the thick door. Impatiently she called again. "Hello?"

Giving up, she eased the door open. Surprisingly, the massive door swung nimbly underhand. Giving the interior a quick but thorough scan, she noted not even a candle glowed. *Poor man. The shepherd must be too injured to move enough to light a candle.* Sympathy filled her soft voice, "Hello?" Pausing, she waited, hoping for even the slightest sound.

Nothing.

The desire to find the injured Shepherd overrode caution. After allowing her body to follow her head into the room, she eased the door shut. Remaining stationary allowed her vision to adjust to the murky darkness. Still, it was hard to find her patient in the dim expanse. Listening for any response, she dropped the heavy backpack onto the floor and called again, "Hello?"

A sudden whoosh roared in her ears, the sound cutting the stillness. Lia didn't have time to figure out where it came from, or what it was before her right hand was jerked straight up. *What? What's going on?*

An involuntary grunt ripped from her lungs as she was yanked into the middle of the vast space. The movement was so fast Lia had no idea how she'd ended up halfway across the room, her feet dragging behind her. *How did I... My wrist, it's caught... Got to free it.* Lia's eyes widened at the sight of the leather binding on her wrist now hanging above her head.

Her bound wrist.

How did it get up there?

Instinctively she reacted, struggling to pull it down while reaching up to untangle her captured hand. As soon as her free hand lifted, it, too, was caught in the same manner.

Immediately, Lia found herself up on her tiptoes as a coil of leather rope held both her hands captive, up and over her head. She stared at her bound hands, her mouth rounding to a perfect o. *Impossible. Utterly Impossible. How? Why?* Questions exploded inside her head. None explained a way out of the tether binding her wrists.

"Hey," she shouted frantically at nothing. "What's going on?" Her head swiveled left, right, and then left again, trying to get a glimpse of her captor. *Where are they?* Panic swept all through her, making her voice high, shrill and tight. "What are you doing?

What's going on? Why are you doing this!" She struggled, tugging hard against the bonds, but they held fast, digging in and cutting skin.

Liquid oozed a slow path down her forearm. Blood.

Lia knew it was blood because it was warm. Even amid the alarm flooding her brain, the smell was distinctly metallic.

Oh God. That's my blood.

Her stomach lurched, protesting the sudden onslaught of bile filling her throat. Full body tremors shook her. *What's going on? Why is this happening? What am I going to do? Good God in heaven, please help me. Why would anyone do this? To me? What could they possibly want?*

She had to calm down. Forcing air into her gasping lungs was a struggle.

Anger helped. A trace of irritation cut into the panic in her voice. "What's going on? Why are you doing this?" Anxiously searching the room proved futile for it appeared empty, although a slight, barely perceptible noise stated otherwise. Straining hard to hear over her pounding heart rewarded her efforts with one soft sound, the scuff of a boot, maybe?

"Who's there?" The panic in her voice rose to one notch below terrified. It jumped to petrified when there was no sound, much less an answer. "What do you want with me?" she cried.

Silence stretched.

Abruptly, the front of her dress tightened against her trachea, practically slitting her throat. The sound of a blade being unsheathed filled the silence. Lia lost her breath. Even before she could brace herself for the impact of steel, there was a loud, long rip.

The gown instantly puddled at her toes.

It didn't have the decency to float down, or even drift. One minute she was clothed and respectable---the next, utterly exposed and vulnerable. A deep baritone gasp sounded behind her and suddenly Lia's eyes opened. She hadn't known she had shut them until they'd flown open. Instinctively one knee shot up and her hands tried vainly to swoop down to cover her nakedness. The inability heightened an already alarming awareness in the futility of her situation.

A growl rising from the depths of her throat morphed into a manic cry.

Lia screamed at her attacker. "What do you want with me? Why are you doing this? Who are you?" She raged on, but her screaming words became incomprehensible, sounding more like the roar of a wounded animal than a terrified and furious human being.

The strangled shouts didn't prompt a single word of explanation. Lia continued to rage, but saving her voice, she did so inwardly and focused on the need to hold the threatening tears in check. *I will not let them see me cry.*

Releasing an unconsciously held breath, Lia concentrated on escape.

Even if it meant leaving both hands behind.

She twisted and tugged. Long legs pumped air. She writhed, wrenching desperately at her ties. She squirmed and yanked. Her heart raced, pounding with rage. Lia struggled violently, ignoring the pain and damage she was inflicting on herself.

"Stop." A deep, dictatorial voice barked the single command.

Lia barely heard the order above the blood pounding in her ears.

But her body did, and she stilled. Blood streamed down both arms, flowing freely down each curvaceous side, steadily inching down the length of her bare outer thighs. A heavy silence ensued, interrupted only by her ragged breaths and a steady drip. Blood dripping. Despair hit and a sob threatened, her pleas sounded strangled.

She barely choked out, "Why are you doing this?" Desperation filled her dwindling voice. "What do you want?" *Please don't hurt me. Please. Don't.*

No answer.

"What do you want with me?" The whispered plea remained unanswered. She tried again. "Why won't you answer me?"

Maybe it was the long, frightening silence that ensued after her tirade.

Or maybe it was the overwhelming desire to be free, but she needed information if there was any hope of escape and this was getting her nowhere. Straightening her spine, she proclaimed, "I'm an American citizen. My government knows I'm in this area and will come looking when I don't report in tomorrow." Not exactly the truth, but her captor wasn't privy to that little tidbit. "They will find me. You will be held accountable for this." She swallowed big, garnering a little courage. "They will hunt you to the ends of the world if you hurt me."

Silence.

A slow, encompassing rage began to supplant the terror. Indignation coated her words, which grated out from behind clenched teeth. "Whatever it is you want from me, I'll do it. I'll get it." Frantically her head swiveled back and forth, searching for her attacker. "But I can't, if you don't tell me what it is you want." She waited, hoping, praying for an answer. *Please. Just say whatever it is you want so I can do it and leave. Please.*

Lia waited until she couldn't stand the silence any longer. Anger clipped her speech, punching each word into a stiff staccato. "Why are you doing this? What in the world do you want from me?" After waiting a moment for a nonexistent answer, she rushed on. "I don't have any money. No one is going to pay for my ransom. I don't know who you think I am, but you've made a mistake. A terrible mistake. I'm not whoever you think I am."

Releasing an exasperated sigh accomplished nothing. Lia forged on, hoping against hope the truth would literally set her free. "I'm only here because we received word a goat herder had taken a nasty fall down the side of a mountain and needed medical treatment and I was the only one available. Omar, my usual guide, couldn't come. There wasn't anyone else and the boy who delivered the distress call said Khalid, the shepherd, couldn't be moved down the mountain to the clinic where I work. I was the only one available to come and treat his injuries and…" Lia grabbed a quick breath as her speech trailed off, her oxygen supply completely used up. The lack of response prompted repetition of the single most important factor in her discourse. "I was the only one available." A pause produced nothing. "The only one." Her voice faded away until silence, again, filled the air.

Lia wiggled her fingers, striving to pump blood back into them, wanting the tingling to disappear. Sneaking a quick look behind both her shoulders still hadn't revealed her captor's identity or his presence. But a rustling sound caught her attention. It could have been anything, even just the brush of fabric against fabric. Knowing someone could hear incited another question. "What can you possibly hope to gain by kidnapping me? I'm nobody." Anguish filled her tone. "I'm only a humble relief worker. A volunteer. I work for Global Outreach. We're a nonprofit organization and don't have any money." Her tone lowered, full of misery. "And if you think all Americans are rich, well, you can rule that out. My parents aren't even comfortable. They're middle class. Lower middle class." She waited a moment before explaining, "They don't have any money either."

No answer. No commentary. Nothing.

"Look. I don't know what you want, but you're going to have to tell me what it is so I can help you get it. Savvy?" Wincing at the pain in both wrists halted her request and she quit prying at the leather strips holding her immobile. Deepening lacerations verified all her previous efforts to slip out of the bindings were not only futile but damaging.

All she could do was yell, so she did, venting all her frustration in her raised voice. "What *Is* your problem? Can't you answer me? Why won't you answer? Just one question. Just one."

Fear stank and she reeked of it. Lia knew it and hated it. *If only he'd tell me what he wants.* She could face anything—if she just knew what it was. Curbing the desire to beg literally left a bad taste in her mouth, for she'd bit her lip to the point of blood to keep from pleading. Desperation turned her legs to jelly and her body sank toward the floor.

"Arhhh." Lia's wail of pain suddenly filled the soundless room. Immediately she stiffened. A white-hot fire blazed in her wrists and Lia shot to her tiptoes, frantic to take the weight off her injuries. But it didn't matter. Her struggles had only tightened the restraints, knitting them deeper into widening gashes. She could barely breathe, the pain knifing through her, making her gasp wildly. Once opened, her mouth turned traitor. "Please let me go." Her voice sounded desperate and hoarse, even to her. But she couldn't help it.

Again, she implored. "Please?"

Lia waited.

Silence.

Pain reduced her to her worst fear.

She begged, her voice only a shredded whisper. "Please cut me down." *Please. Oh God. Please let me go.* "Please let me go."

No answer.

"Please?" Her voice barely held back a sob. Her eyelids sealed for the tiniest moment before they blinked rapidly. The burn of unshed tears threatened to overwhelm even the pain. *I will not cry. I will not cry.*

She heard footsteps.

Suddenly a door opened and then closed.

Silence.

Lia fought panic and forced her mind to focus. From her vantage point, escape appeared impossible for the empty room held nothing to aid any attempt. *Somebody please help me.* Terror gripped her, suddenly all too tangible and unbearably overwhelming.

Lia froze as a soft whoosh of air stirred, sending the distinctly musty smell of time and ages swirling up to her. The soft sounds of the night, the rustle of wind among trees, along with the crickety chirp of insects floated in before suddenly cut off by the thud of a closing door.

Lia didn't wait for whatever was coming next. "What do you want?" With a massive effort, she managed to keep most of the panic out of her voice. "What do you want with me?"

Silence.

Why wouldn't he answer? The depth of his previous one-syllable demand proved his gender.

Still no answer. The silence was broken by the sound of fabric ripping. Her brows knotted and the furrows in her forehead deepened. Long, suspenseful moments translated into terrifying clarity when something icy touched her. Lia involuntarily sucked in her breath before a soft, short wail escaped her. Her body jerked as something frozen swept down the length of her arm. She gritted her teeth to keep silent, but her body refused to still.

Good God, that's cold.

Tears spilled from her eyes. She wasn't crying, but her eyes watered from the pain. The pain in her wrists and arms magnified with every shiver. She couldn't stop the shivers. Lia begged, her voice wobbly, breathless. "Stop. Please." Regardless, the ministrations continued. Still she pleaded, "Oh God, please stop." Her body became one giant spasm.

Lia closed her eyes. Somehow the agony worsened. Opening her eyes, she focused on one of the intersections of the hand-planed boards on the far wall. Never feeling the tears sliding down her cheeks, Lia soon became aware that all the concentration in the world wasn't going to diminish the hurt being forced upon her physical body.

The pain grew intolerable. Lia forgot to stretch up on her toes. Her body sagged. Suffering made her voice crack as she continued to murmur words she no longer expected an answer to, but the words tumbled out for it was all she wanted. All she would ever want again. Incoherently, she begged. "Please. Please stop. Just... stop, please."

Her voice faded.

Pain won. "Plea..."

Lia passed out.

Silence again reigned.

Two

Mute Worthen continued to bathe the unconscious woman, washing the blood from her arms and sides. Each stroke grew increasingly rough for he fought a strange urge to yield to her pleas for release. Not to mention his brewing rage at showing even a single sign of weakness.

Allowing that one tiny gasp of surprise, or was it admiration, to escape wasn't his usual M.O. Outbursts of any kind wasn't something he allowed himself. Not even when faced with the perfection of one Lia Von Stratham.

Von Stratham's photo hadn't been included in Mission Intel. It hadn't been necessary. Regardless, and in no way fathomable, could that be considered an excuse. Mute stiffened with resolve, silently vowing not to react again.

His gaze indolently traveled over the goddess dangling before him, automatically homing in on that sexy little mole hovering above full, sumptuous lips. Mute stared at the unconscious woman far too long.

Then he utilized his should-be-patented mental sequencing system, perfected by years of practice, to ignore a growing desire. Gnawing on every piece of information assimilated about this mission, he categorized the Intel.

In order of acquisition.
Then, in order of importance.
And then, in order of completion.

It kept his mind occupied while he cleaned, salved, and bandaged the prisoner's injuries. His employer wanted Ms. Von Stratham healthy, a condition he actually preferred. Transporting dead or near-death prisoners made travel difficult.

Not for the first time since he'd accepted this assignment, a sense of unease filled him. Something about Marcel DuPries set off his internal alarm. Still, DuPries' reasons for kidnapping Von Stratham appeared rational. And the fee was very, very handsome.

The woman had stolen a 'private' file. The need to retrieve it warranted Lia's abduction. Still, questioning a client's motivation came naturally to Mute. Trust was not only impossible in his line of work, it could kill you.

Mute's shoulders tensed and it took some effort to relax them. Still, the frown on his lips refused to go away.

Roughly, without regard to the prisoner's well-being, he finished the task even as his mind worked on the million-dollar question. Did he believe his employer? Did Von Stratham steal from DuPries? If so, where was the disk?

He threw the bloody water out the back door and put up the wash pan he'd used. A quick glance at her bandages communicated all he needed to know. Von Stratham wasn't in any danger of bleeding to death.

With first aid accomplished, Mute returned to his assignment, ignoring the rest of her.

That impossibly perfect rest of her.

Knowing he had to be completely in charge of himself, he focused on her injuries and his handiwork. The blood had quit seeping, the crude dressings on her wrists proving adequate.

Mute considered cutting her loose for she would eventually regain consciousness. Her wounds would probably reopen if she tried to escape again.

Not if.

When.

Letting his gaze travel the entire length of the naked woman dangling before him, Mute's blood heated. Automatically he disregarded it, pushing it aside with practiced determination. His eyes locked on the birthmark positively identifying his captive.

A tiny blush red mark rested at the top curve of her left, and admittedly, perfect butt cheek. The right half of an X slashed through a tiny crescent shape---the mark guaranteeing an extremely generous fee.

Odd. It looked more like a tattoo for the edges were crisp and deliberate. Finding his fingertips mere millimeters from touching it, he marveled how his hand had gotten there. Deliberately he lowered it.

Was she cold?

Where the hell had that come from? Mute shook his head to clear it. Mission perimeters didn't include prisoner comfort.

Never had.

Never would.

He had only stripped Von Stratham to verify the birthmark. Mute's gaze fell to her backpack, of which he had the contents emptied and categorized within minutes.

No clothes.

Something about the packing made him question the competency of its owner. Okay, it held enough food for two people for days. However, the fact most of it was perishable begged for answers. Was she planning on meeting someone? Were they coming here? Or did she plan on roughing it by steering clear of towns or people for a time? If so, essential equipment, such as basic camping gear or even rudimentary supplies, was missing.

Nonetheless, she hadn't packed any other clothes. Only medical supplies and food. A soft, barely audible curse crossed thinned lips. Resolutely Mute dug into his own pack and pulled out an extra pair of jeans and a T-shirt.

Changing his mind, he stuffed the shirt back in the bag. His frown deepened, surpassing his customary scowl, landing on a full-fledged grimace. Pulling a T-shirt over tied, strung hands would be impossible. However, reasoning pants were better than nothing at all, he moved to accomplish the job. Mute lifted each delicate foot and stuffed long, shapely legs into the denims, keeping his eyes averted as much as possible.

Normally he would be happy to indulge in what were perks of the trade, but right now he didn't want to deal with the ache of a hard-on.

But it didn't matter.

Blood zinged south the instant his knuckles brushed the soft, warm skin of her abdomen while zipping the pants. Mute fumbled with the closure, curbing the instinct to swear under his breath.

"Damn." The curse exploded only seconds later when his pants slid down those endless legs, exposing every gorgeous inch of her again. He refused to allow his admiring gaze to follow.

Sort of.

Ignoring his groin, Mute stomped to his pack and pulled out a length of rope. Flipping out a knife, he decisively cut off a piece before stalking back and sliding the pants up again, deftly tying them in place. Although her comatose body jerked with each harsh movement, it in no way salved his ache. Muttering under his breath, he heaped every bit of his anger with his own reaction onto the woman. Enough that her unconscious body jerked with every pull and tug.

He cursed at himself and the ineptness of his prisoner---who apparently hadn't the sense God gave a goose if she didn't even carry a change of clothes.

Mute stepped back. Placing large, competent hands on lean hips, he studied his hostage, and then the room. Remembering a stack of wool blankets in a cabinet from an earlier search, he retrieved one and quickly cut a hole in the middle. Anger kept him focused on the important task of eliminating distraction. At least until Mute stood in front of his captive, holding the blanket up.

Even though bound hands stretched Von Stratham taller than actual height, he towered over her petite and curvaceous frame. Tendrils of dark honey hair escaped a low ponytail, framing sculpted cheekbones. Though his captive remained comatose, worry lines seamed a broad, translucent forehead above delicately arched brows. Long dark eyelashes draped radiant skin. Her full lips were parted, capturing his attention. Or was it that tiny mole perched seductively above a sensuous upper lip?

Mute's heart beat hitched up a notch as his gaze lazed over her long, delicate throat, drifting down feminine shoulders. And then it pounded, punching into his chest wall as his stare traveled across a tantalizingly delicious looking collarbone before skimming luscious, perfect breasts. His head reflexively dipped, his mouth opening, itching to take in each succulent nipple and taste her.

Catching himself in time, he forced his hands to place the blanket over her head, letting it drop over her shoulders. Careful not to touch those enticing curves, he smoothed the coarse fabric in place. Raised arms prevented it from covering her completely but in this case, less was definitely more.

He stepped back, adjusted his lower self for his own body seemed hell bent on annoying him, before moving away from the temptation of Ms. Lia Von Stratham.

Intent on catching twenty winks, he unrolled his sleeping bag on an old straw mattress in a nearby empty room. One far enough away to thwart temptation but close enough to hear any escape attempt. He lay down and closed his eyes. Several long minutes passed.

"Dammit." The sharp, low curse surprised even Mute.

Rising, he retrieved the pan he'd used earlier, not allowing himself to ask why. Stomping back to his prisoner, he set the bowl upside-down on the floor and gently placed each of her small sandaled feet on top of it. *Now she wouldn't dangle.*

Mute slipped back to his bed and, again, fell atop the meager mattress, willing his brain to shut down. At least the thinking part.

That always vigilant component never slept.

It took a full minute. Forty seconds longer than normal. Two hours later, Mute woke.

Instantly alert, he listened to the night. Whispered grunts and an almost imperceptible creaking spoke volumes. Mute closed his eyes, wanting sleep again. Von Stratham's attempts to escape would prove futile.

But rest eluded him. Picturing her struggles ran like scenes of a nightmare in his head, evoking the damage she was inflicting with every pull and twist. Every painful gasp sucked from her lungs, every wince, every tortured groan, only ingrained the images deep within his mind. Real effort kept him from calling out to her to cease her struggles. It took an even greater strength to unclench his tight jaw, but that resolve had no effect on his tense muscles.

Finally, the sounds of struggling stopped. *Good. She's passed out again.*

He closed his eyes. Surprisingly, his body relaxed. His mind certainly didn't. A grudging admiration for the slight beauty stole up on him for she hadn't cried out. Not once.

And it had to hurt.

Really, really hurt. Leather burns hurt like hell. And her shoulders had to be on fire by now. Still, she fought to escape.

Mute heard a drip. Before he could determine the origin, another drip sounded. Realization washed over him and an audible curse erupted from his lips.

Suddenly a loud gasp sounded from the main room. *No, she hadn't passed out. She was wide awake. And she heard me.* Quiet no longer held any merit, so he disregarded it.

Mute leaped up, storming toward his captive. Each step of his boots sounded like thunder on the cold, stony floor. With lightning ferocity, he swiped at her torso, swinging her around to face him, his dark eyes commanding even more than his roar. "Stop!"

Wild, crazed eyes focused on him. Her face was filled with primal terror, but there was also a question. Remarkably, Von Stratham obeyed.

He wondered if she knew how her short, shallow pants thundered in the unforgiving silence. At least, she remained still, seemingly paralyzed.

Waiting.

Understanding dawned and Mute's broad shoulders relaxed slightly. His dark eyes threatened, but his tone neutralized. "I'm not going to hurt you."

Her chin jutted up even as her eyes narrowed. A short, staccato breath exploded from her thinned lips.

The scowl on his face softened into a frown. "Haven't been paid to."

Inch by slow inch, her horror lessened. Wariness replaced the terror.

That apprehension morphed into anger, which grew and fermented. Mute stood transfixed by the degrees of her emotion. He couldn't look away.

Her eyes sliced his with their ferocity.

Fury began to fill them. And then.

Rage.

Amber eyes brightened as the anger mutated into a Wrath-of-God madness.

No, more than amber. They were a dark tawny gold, almost translucent, but brimming with fire. Fully on fire. Filled with passion. Filled with Life.

For the first time in his thirty-three years, Mute couldn't catch even the tiniest breath. Although the wealth of his captive's vehemence concentrated solely on his immediate and total demise, the depth of it overwhelmed him.

Never had he witnessed a passion of such intensity before. The scope… that realm… this fervent desire for just living was unheard of, unimaginable in his world.

Something buried deep within Mute snapped fully awake, as if leaping from long suppressed depths. His usually lethargic gaze widened slightly for three, maybe four long seconds, before resuming its usual cynical slit. His lips flattened into a single line, desperate to control the sentiment suddenly raging within him.

Mute was not prepared for emotion. Hell, sentimentality didn't exist for him. Feeling wasn't something he'd ever dealt with before. Long ago, he'd categorized emotion as strictly baggage, refusing to accept or deal with something so trivial. A decision he had never questioned.

Had never had reason to question.

Until.

Lia Von Stratham.

Three

Oh.
My.
God.
Please help me.

Lia's mouth moved as she prayed, but no sound came out. Her previously unseen captor was terror personified. She wasn't sure she didn't prefer his earlier invisibility. The man was huge. Dark. Wicked.

A surge of energy pulsed through her, the desire to escape suddenly paramount and again Lia fought, struggling desperately against her bonds.

"Stop!" That voice was as dangerous as the man.

His black scowl and annoyed stance only cemented Lia's horror. Her muddled brain barely understood this particular devil wanted compliance.

Or at the very least, obedience.

Something in Lia protested and again she flailed against the ties binding her. Now that she no longer felt the need to remain silent, a desperate cry escaped. Still, all the thrashing in the world wouldn't release her from the restraints.

The realization slowly sank in. The knowledge she would bleed to death if she didn't stop struggling prompted her to obey the harsh command, whether she wanted to or not. Her long, low wail, sounding traitorously defeated, echoed in the cavernous room.

Lia lost her breath and all ability to move any and every muscle. The finality of imminent, impending death struck home. Hot tears threatened and Lia clamped her eyes shut, forcing the waterworks away. She would never give the brute in front of her the satisfaction.

Gulping big for it was impossible to tamp down so much sensation, Lia turned her head away, letting it hang.

But she wouldn't cry.

Not in this life time.

This enemy would never see tears.

Ever.

She tensed as he unwound the bandages, inspecting the new damage. It galled her when he took his time reapplying the wrappings. Lia forced her body to remain still. It took everything in her, for when the task was finished he, again, cleaned the fresh blood from her arms and sides. Her only saving grace came in the form of an inaudible chant. Or was it a prayer? *This isn't happening. This isn't happening. This isn't happening.*

Lia remained silent, ignoring the chill seeping through her skin. She only wanted her captor to go away. To leave.

She wondered at the reasons behind his administrations. The logical part of her brain told her he was only following orders to bring her in unharmed. But she had no idea who had given the orders. Or what the stipulations, if any, were. He could have as easily been told to kill her. Even now, she had no idea what he wanted from her.

Or why she was now his prisoner.

One possibility was mistaken identity, making her wrongly convicted for actions she hadn't committed. The knowledge irked her to no end, enough that her body automatically jerked slightly with the injustice of it all. Her dry tongue stuck to the roof of her mouth even as her glare threatened to reduce him to nothingness.

Being held captive infuriated her. Being held captive for no reason enraged her. She opened her mouth to rail at her captor, but the instant she looked into his eyes her mother's voice suddenly, abruptly, shouted inside her head.

Lia lost all ability to speak.

Lost the capacity to breathe.

And lost herself in those empty eyes.

Her gaze remained as captive as she was while her mother's description of the color black echoed over and over in her mind, sounding like a looped tape recording of her lessons. Her mother's voice insistent, but factual, flatly repeating over and over the specifics of endless painting classes.

Black is not a real color, but rather the absence of color. Black doesn't exist. Black is nothingness.

Lia finally got it.

Now, at this instant, the concept of black sank in.

Lia understood.

Those glaring black eyes staring into hers, although insistent, were void.

Dark and empty.

A shiver traveled down her spine for the term *soulless* came to mind. It took a monumental effort to look away.

Only the pain wracking her body focused her fury once again.

Oh, how it hurt. It was entirely possible the only part of her that didn't hurt was a quarter sized spot just behind her right ear. She wanted to cringe. She wanted to cry. She wanted to wail.

She wanted answers.

Her voice was choked with pain and fury, the decibel level through the roof. "I have nothing. Nothing of importance." Her hard gaze remained defiantly fixed on her indifferent captor. Purposely she didn't struggle against her restraints, trying to project a sense of tolerance. "And I am not wealthy. There's no chance of a ransom."

His disinterested features remained devoid of emotion. Even his tone personified impersonal. "You underestimate your worth."

Lia's frown hardened into a fierce scowl. "You've got the wrong person."

He didn't answer for the longest time. Finally, he spoke. "No." The man merely made a statement, his voice lethargic, even though it conveyed absolute certainty.

"What do you plan to do with me?" She wasn't convinced she really wanted to know.

"Turn you over to my employer. What else?" His body language implied a languid disconnection to this assignment. To her.

"And what if I promised to double the offer?" She didn't have the money, but did he know that?

"Uh un." His shrug of denial was hardly a movement at all. Regardless, those black eyes remained blank.

It would be impossible to convince this man he had the wrong woman, so she didn't try. Lia hated what she was thinking, hated even more the question tripping off her tongue. "What would it take? If not money, then what?" Her voice trailed off until it was barely audible.

One dark, thick eyebrow cocked at an unnaturally high angle on his otherwise unfathomable face. Full lips set in a hard, forced line. Fine lines crinkled the corners of narrowed eyes.

Lia wondered if the devil himself had sired this one. His hard face was all angles and planes. Shadowed and dark. Square. Tough. A short pony tail of dark hazel hair hung from the back of his neck, empathizing those deep-set eyes. A few strands too short to stay tucked in place hung around his face. Although they held only a hint of wave, his masculine features contrasted so drastically they appeared to curl. Days old stubble on a chiseled jaw only accentuated his essence.

Danger.

In capital letters.

Those black, fathomless eyes seared her to her toes.

Lia inhaled. Regardless of how much he terrified her, she wouldn't ask again. At least not right now. Stubborn determination and resolve demanded she grow a pair. Her chin lifted, jutting up as she waited for his answer.

After giving her the merest glance, the tyrant visually dismissed her, returning his attention to putting up the remaining medical supplies.

The silence lengthened.

Still, Lia had to question his motive. Had to know. Breathlessly she asked, "Why are you doing this?" She raised her face, drilling him with her persistence. "What would anyone want with me? I'm nobody." A vacantness crept into her tone. "Nobody at all."

His face remained expressionless, although his eyes filled with an intensity that seemed foreign.

Lia stared, as if she couldn't look away, waiting for his answer.

Finally, she blinked.

Immediately, his intense gaze dropped.

Had there, for a scant moment, been something in those black eyes, or was she imagining it?

Abruptly he appeared released. Only God knew from what. He shrugged, indifference again written all over him. "Doesn't matter." His voice lazed over the words as if he truly didn't know. Or care.

Lia was getting tired of this roller coaster of emotions she was riding. Terror. Anger. And then horror. Suddenly an all-consuming volatile fury erupted within her, the depth of it fully apparent as she screamed at the top of her lungs. "Who hired you?"

Silence.

She raged on. "Why me? What do you want with me? What do they want? Are you taking me somewhere or what?" Lia grabbed a quick breath to replenish her sudden lack of oxygen. "How much are they paying you? Do you even know who hired you? Are you going to..."

"Quiet!" His harsh tone demanded immediate compliance.

Lia had no intention of obeying. Her frown deepened as did the wrinkles etched onto her forehead. "I don't think so. Not until I get some answers, you scum sucking, sorry, vile…" She hurried to think of adequately lethal descriptions of her captor, finally settling on, "Bastard. At the very least I deserve answers." Daggers shot from her eyes even as her voice pummeled him furiously. "If you think you're going to get...

"Yeowww." Lia let out a howl when her head was yanked back. Strong fingers had gathered deep against her scalp, pulling her head back. Lia's watering eyes locked with his. And with the last ounce of common sense within her, she immediately accepted his dominance.

Her eyes lowered. She refused to question how sick her compliance was. But her body remained stiff, managing a tenuous grasp on what little insolence she could muster.

"Shhh." His voice was low, but there was no mistaking the menace behind the command. This man expected to be obeyed. His fingers tightened even further as he held her immobile. His lips flattened to a snarl as he postured threateningly over her.

Unconsciously, Lia whimpered a soft little sound.

She couldn't help it. Her captor was utterly menacing. So deadly looking. So evil. Those fierce black eyes promised retribution. More terrifying was the chilling readiness of his solid form. Everything about him, his tense body, his resolved gaze, the dark power within him, promised the ultimate penalty if she disobeyed. His stance was ready, waiting, even though he still had one hand tied up in her hair.

Her strangled whimper only made those dark eyes harden. Already thinned lips flattened, while his muscles bunched, ready.

No, this man didn't have a sensitive side, much less in touch with it.

Lia swallowed big, her mouth dry as sand. She managed to keep silent, but couldn't help when her eyes widened with absolute fear. Hiding the terror pouring from her was impossible. However, she finally managed to shrug one shoulder enough to make it appear she was pulling out of his grasp instead of him letting go. She garnered strength when his hand moved away from her. Insolence replaced the terror in her gold eyes as she forced herself to stare back.

Lia gulped again, fighting for, at the very least, the semblance of bravery. "What do you want?" Depths previously untapped kept her voice steady. Her chin jutted up. "Really? What do you expect to gain by this?" She gave him what she hoped was a quelling stare even as her insides quaked.

Something flickered in those hard eyes as he continued to lock glares with her. Lia, at first, thought it might be respect, but decided it was only wariness. Nevertheless, the man wasn't talking. She would have to nudge the info out of him. Opening her mouth to remind him, the stony look he shot her made her think twice. She didn't get a chance to say anything for her captor suddenly spun and strode away, toward an open door leading somewhere. The abruptness startled Lia.

"Wait!" She hesitated, and then added a soft, "Please?" After a long moment of waiting, an exasperated sigh escaped. Unconsciously her body sagged low before it went rigid as the pain knifed into her wrists again---wrists already inflamed from previous torture. Refusing to acknowledge the pain, she focused her attention on the man who'd halted but hadn't turned to face her.

Lia pleaded, "Please, just tell me what you want with me."

He didn't answer. He just stood there, contemplating the floor.

Lia waited, but he didn't speak. Or move. Resignation set in, allowing her to accept his silence. Lia slumped, the breath leaking away from her lungs, her head drooping.

Finally, he turned back to her. "Nothing." He paused, the moment lengthening, his gaze studying her shocked expression. "But my employer does." Black eyes stared into hers.

For a split second, something blazed in them.

Then abruptly---nothing.

Utterly no emotion. In his eyes or his voice. It was as if she, nor he, existed.

Lia wanted desperately to exist. To survive. To live. To just be. Her voice dripped with despair. "Why does your employer want me?"

"You have something he wants." The conviction in his voice squashed any doubt she'd entertained about persuading him to simply let her go when he knew the truth.

"But I don't." Lia frantically searched her brain for anything. Anything someone might construe as valuable. She couldn't think of a thing she owned that would interest a single solitary soul, other than herself. Her tone screamed puzzled. "There's my backpack. Take anything you want." Her nodding head indicated both her pack and her desire for him to inspect it.

"I've already gone through it. It's not there." His black eyes darkened and his tone dropped half an octave, delving deeper than deep should get. A flame touched his eyes for a moment before they again hardened into unfathomable depths. "And you're not hiding it on your person."

Lia felt her cheeks burn. Automatically her gaze dropped to the floor, but she curbed her embarrassment. This was no time to wallow in mortification. Priority had to be getting out of this mess. Facing him, she huffed out her best impression of seething indignation, "No I'm not. I don't have anything of value. I don't own anything important." Her brows knotted and her voice implored. "Who said I did?"

He shrugged. "Marcel DuPries".

Delicate brows dipped as intense puzzlement flooded her expression. "Never heard of him." Her heart sank. "I don't recognize the name." When no answer was forthcoming, she drank in a lung-filling breath, trying to quell the sudden misgivings. After a moment of silence, she asked, "What am I supposed to have possession of?"

"A disk."

She repeated the question. "A disk?" When he only nodded, she prodded for more. "What kind of disk?"

"The kind that stores information." He spoke slowly as if she were a child.

Lia could never accept sarcasm well. She snapped back. "Yeah. I know. I meant what kind. As in micro disk? Flash drive? ICD?" Had her hands been free she'd have been tempted to knock a tap or two on his forehead.

His frown was ugly and dark. "Just a disk."

"What's supposed to be on this disk?"

He hesitated so long she was afraid he wasn't going to tell her. Finally, he stated, "You stole a file Monsieur DuPries considers…" His pause was eloquent. "Private."

Lia unconsciously shook her head. "No. I told you. I don't know anyone by that name."

He turned, moving away. "Whatever you say." Lia recognized the dismissal in the apathetic tone.

She urgently yelled at him. "HEY! Wait." It was apparent the man was losing patience by his rigid stance and cold expression. "You know I don't have any disk. You can let me go. I can't give you something I don't have."

He didn't move. Not a single muscle twitched anywhere on his person, but Lia got the feeling he was laughing at her. Yet, his voice remained neutral. "Well, I could torture you until you tell me where it is, *or...*" He hesitated. Lia paled, for she knew unequivocally he could and probably would. "I can deliver you to DuPries." His shoulder lifted in the barest of shrugs.

Lia's body sagged for a full minute before her backbone stiffened. "I honestly have no idea who DuPries is or why anyone would think I stole anything. Anything at all." Her voice deepened, truth seeping throughout every syllable. "I've never stolen anything in my entire life."

He stared at her for so long she felt as if time itself stopped. Abruptly he straightened. "Whatever you say." He headed for the door as if he hadn't a care in the world.

Lia let him go. It was no use talking to him. The man didn't believe a word she said. Although she understood the doubt and his questions, it still hurt he didn't care enough to discover the truth.

The truth about her. She bit her bottom lip, unintentionally hard.

She had to get out of here.

Tugging tentatively against her restraints, she groaned. Oh Man, it hurt. The pain was excruciating, but the emotional ache was unbearable. Her heart had never been prepared for this kind of damage. She'd been raised to uphold the goodness of man.

All of man.

And now that trust had been breached. A child of innocence could never accept such treachery.

A tear slipped down her cheek. And then another, on the opposite cheek.

Lia clenched her teeth until they threatened to break, the grinding of them painful, as if her jaws were going to crack under the pressure.

She would not cry. Not now, not ever. Her eyes burned, but she held the tears back. Lia focused, trying desperately to figure out an escape plan.

Resolutely, she tried to think about the best ways she could free herself. As she studied on the problem, it seemed her best chance would be after her kidnapper cut her loose.

And eventually, the man would have to if he was going to deliver her to DuPries, whoever DuPries was. Lia closed her eyes, concentrating, trying to access her memory for anything possibly resembling a stolen disk. Or an unknown French man. Nothing came to mind. She couldn't attach any memory to anything French or to any file. She didn't know any French men. Or women, for that matter. She was only your typical Global Outreach worker who'd spent the last few months vaccinating children. Not an international spy. It was inconceivable anyone could think otherwise. She lost all sense of time as she pondered the situation.

Lia suddenly found herself falling, gasping loudly as her arms dropped. Searing pain shot through her shoulders. A gut-wrenching moan tore from her lips. Unable to gain her balance, she teetered. A hard hand settled around one shoulder, steadying her. She looked at it, and then found its owner.

Her eyes narrowed of their own accord, her chin tilting up.

The beast had cut her down, but before she could move, he had swung both of her arms behind her back, securing her wrists, again, with the tether. Blood and sensation poured into her fingers. Seconds later, her arms were on fire all the way to her fingernails. She bit back a cry as she flexed her fingers, trying to lessen the pain.

Hell filled her veins as feeling returned. Her stifled cry reverberated in the silence.

"The intensity will decrease in a minute." He was watching her closely, those black, hard eyes studying her. Lia fought the pain, finding just enough strength to glare back at him. His words belied his obvious lack of concern. He moved from her, gathering her pack and then strapping it to her back. It took several long and uncomfortable moments, for he had to undo the buckles completely before strapping it in position between her shoulder blades, and then refastening the clasps again. It was awkward and in an ungainly position since her restrained hands rested on the bottom of it.

She gave him an incredulous look, momentarily forgetting her pain. And her predicament. "Surely you don't expect me to walk like this?"

"I expect you to run if I tell you to." His answer came without even a second's hesitation. He threw her a quelling glance before packing his own bag. Hoisting the duffle onto his back, he adjusted it until it lay between his broad shoulders the way he wanted.

He held something in his hand as he started toward her.

Lia took a step back. He was coming for her, moving ever closer. Her feet stumbled upon themselves as she desperately continued backing away, terror seeping from every pore.

His eyes hardened, glinting real steel as his hand snaked out, wrapping her upper arm with an inescapable grip. "Drink," he commanded. He lifted a water bottle.

Lia remained paralyzed.

When she didn't move, he reached for her head. Latching onto her face, his fingers dug into the sides of her cheeks. She tried to escape, but it was no use. She was held immobile. Her mouth involuntarily opened, for he was already pouring water between her lips. She gulped the water because she had to breathe right then.

Suddenly she couldn't remember anything ever tasting so wonderful. The liquid was cool, silky, and thirst quenching. Water poured down her chin as well as her throat. And when he lifted the bottle away, Lia tried to catch what was on her face with her tongue. His hesitation was real, his brows knotting somberly, before he again brought the bottle to her lips. The hand on her face dropped and the man seemed to relax the tiniest bit.

Lia drank long, craning in closer. It didn't matter more liquid was on the outside of her than on the inside. She had been thirsty for so long. All night, and had she thought about it, for most of the day before. Her eyes closed as she swallowed the priceless liquid. She was still gulping when he pulled the bottle away, her eyes suddenly open and questioning.

"We need to conserve our supplies." He answered tersely. "You didn't pack the necessities." His voice was gruff and insinuating. "And I didn't pack for two." He took a short pull on the same bottle before capping it and stowing it on his backpack.

Lia didn't like the fact her captor was willing to share germs. It made her uncomfortable. In a very strange way. But she wasn't given time to try to figure out why.

Poking at her backpack, he prodded her to move. "Let's go. We've got a lot of ground to cover." He opened the door slightly, listening to the night. Finally, he motioned for Lia to head out.

"Hey, it's still dark. How are we supposed to see? It's pitch black out there."

His voice lowered, testing the air for sound, while meticulously scanning the open area before them. "We'll be able to see well enough. Just maintain a steady pace." He nudged her across the threshold.

Lia's balance was off, due to the unfamiliarity of having one's hands tied behind her back, and she barely kept from falling. A hot hand on her shoulder held her upright even as it continued to push forward. Lia had no choice but to take a step, then another. And another. To her surprise, her eyes adjusted to the darkness with enough clarity she had no trouble making her way.

They'd covered quite a bit of distance when Lia realized she had no idea where they were going. Or which direction they were taking. She tried to study the stars, remembering what little she had learned about the constellations. She found the North

Star and both Dippers, but that was all she could make out. Lia inwardly cringed at her lack of skill.

Maybe she could pry it out of her captor. "Where are we going?"

He didn't answer.

Lia stopped and, pronouncing each word carefully, asked again, "Where are we going?" This time he, at least, looked at her. She felt more than observed one thick eyebrow cock, as she resisted his firm shove to her shoulder. She had no intention of going anywhere until she got a little information. Her chin lifted a fraction. Then it notched distinctly higher when he still didn't answer.

Lia knew the minute he capitulated, although his expression never changed. Something, she didn't know what, in his manner gave away how little her reaction would matter to him.

"You really don't want to know." His tone was conversational.

"I'm positive I don't." The depth of her reluctance registered in her voice. "I don't even want to go there." Her eyes burned with resentment. "But. You're not giving me a choice and I'm not moving another step until you tell me where you're taking me."

He tensed, fingers curling into his palms. "Keep your voice down." Glancing left and right, he peered into the shadows before again turning his attention to Lia.

Both Lia's eyebrows rose as she waited, silently as requested. She dreaded knowing but needed an answer.

He studied her for a long moment, his lips remaining shut.

Glaring harder, she cocked her head, full lips pursed defiantly.

A full minute passed before he acquiesced. "Baki."

Lia forgot to lower her tone. "What? No way." She gasped loudly, her eyes rounding with surprise. "It's too dangerous." *Good God. Was he crazy?* Americans don't willingly go to Azerbaijan. Okay, so she hadn't volunteered. Lia stole a look at her companion. She could discern his features now that morning was threatening to break. His dark physiognomy could have passed for any number of nationalities. Lia had assumed he was an American, as she was, strictly based on his unaccented English. "Where were you born?" Lia really didn't expect him to answer. Disbelief filled her when he did.

"Michigan."

"Then why are we going where Americans are hated and bombed and prosecuted and stoned and, did I mention, hated?" Obviously, the man hadn't heard about the unrest and the terrorist attacks on Western nationals.

His only response was to shove her forward, moving again. Lia was too upset by his disclosure to resist. He finally spoke, answering her question, but not until they had covered quite a bit of distance. His voice seemed strangled as if, for some unfathomable reason, he was unable to deny her request. "We're making for a private airstrip. From there, we'll fly to Egypt."

Lia was getting a bad feeling. Something about this didn't make sense. Why were they heading east when the destination was west? She glared at him, about to launch into a riled tirade about how this turnip wasn't born yesterday and couldn't accept such a simple explanation when it occurred to her that not knowing his very name put a damper on the derision she so desperately wanted to inflict on him.

And his mother.

Her attempt at disdain didn't exactly sound all that demeaning. "You, you, you… sorry son of a bitch. You're lying." Her lips thinned. "Where are you really taking me?"

His normal bland grimace transformed into a snarl. Lia wanted to shrink away from his irritation, but she didn't. The furious part of her that refused to accept incarceration was the same part refusing to saunter graciously into impending doom. She continued to glare at him even though she had to look away every so often to make sure she didn't stumble or trip. "We're heading south, aren't we?" Lia only knew because it was well past dawn now and the sun was over her left shoulder.

Although technically still morning, it was heating up fast. Mountain deserts were no different than sea level deserts.

Night was cold. Day was hot.

Lia inwardly groaned at the lack of shade in this rocky, barren, grey country. There was little in the way of cover, and it would soon reach the triple digits. Her mouth went dry at the prospect. Lia didn't try to squelch the resentment boiling inside her when she deliberately spun toward her captor, stopping so fast he walked into her. "Why are we going south?" Temper flared in her eyes. Hot. Intense. Desperate. And long overdue.

He jerked back as if punched and a strangled look flashed across his strong face. He stared into her eyes. For a moment, Lia imagined he could see her soul. The force of his gaze hit her head on, causing her to take a step back. His eyes widened slightly before they returned to their usual lackadaisical slits. He raised his hand to once more press her into mobility, but Lia remained stock still, having none of it.

Without thinking of the consequences, she marched into his advance and using her shoulder purposely, she shoved his hand back and away. "Look, whoever you are, I'm not taking another..."

The last thing she saw was the blur of his fist as it swung toward her head.

Four

Damn.

Now he would have to carry her. Resigned, Mute slung the unconscious woman over his shoulder. At least now he could pick up the pace. She weighed nothing.

He frowned. He hadn't wanted to hit her. But the determination in those gorgeous, albeit stubborn eyes insisted she would never have listened to mere words. Luckily, he knew exactly how much force was required to inflict as little damage as possible while attaining the desired results. She'd have a slight headache when she awoke, but there would be no permanent damage.

Mute had to admire her courage. Few stood up to him. And she had actually struck him. Mind you, only with her shoulder, but had her hands been free she would have used them. Had he been one for mirth, he would be chuckling by now at the audacity of her attack. But he wasn't, so his lips remained a flat line.

In fact, it was hard to think at all. He was having major difficulty removing a specific image out of his head. One totally burned into his brain. One literal to him for the fire in her eyes had branded him.

He'd never witnessed such passion before. It had turned her amber eyes so hot they appeared as molten gold. Bright. Liquid. And searing.

Mute shook his head as if to clear it. It was imperative to remain focused on the mission. Everything else was inconsequential, including the zeal and zest of Lia Von Stratham. However, there was a part of him that envied the fervor seething within her. And as much as he didn't want to, he had to respect the iron strength in her spirit. Most women would be nothing more than tearful baggage at this point, but not this one. Von Stratham had actually picked a fight with him. A physical one.

His's lips flicked, but the smile he thought he was making was only an illusion of the mind. It never made it to his face.

Suddenly, the faint crunch, crunch, crunch of approaching feet caught his attention. Automatically he assessed how many, position, and estimated time of arrival. Three. Coming from the South. He had less than two minutes to get out of sight.

Mute scrambled to his only option---a deep ravine eighty yards away. It only took seconds to reach, but it put him within audible range of the approaching men.

He searched for a quiet way down the twelve or so feet to the bottom of the crevice. Loose rock and shale lined the steep sides. Too noisy to slide down and not a goat trail in sight. Time was up so he did the last thing he wanted to do. Mute jumped.

Hitting hard, he fought the instinct to tuck and roll. That feat lost its effectiveness when you were wearing two backpacks as well as an extra person. Landing on the balls of his feet, he kept his knees slightly bent, letting his body absorb most of the shock. Still, Lia's dead weight had lifted when he'd jumped and then landed with a loud thump. He heard her unconscious *whump* when the wind was knocked from her lungs as she bounced onto his rock-hard shoulder.

Mute remained motionless. Listening. The men had stopped, their easy conversation now nonexistent. Of course, they were trying to determine where the noise had come from as well as what or who had made it. He had to get out of sight. Only his training kept the instinctive desire to flee at bay.

Studying the walls of the ravine, Mute spotted what he needed, a small outcropping of rock providing cover from above. Listening to their resumed footsteps and using their noise as cover, he lightly crossed to it, carefully setting his cargo down. He kept his curse inaudible as the realization the brightly-colored blanket serving as Lia's blouse did anything but blend. Using his body, he shielded her from sight.

His own clothing was dark and mottled. As he was big enough to be a screen for her slight form, his camo would do for them both.

The men remained perched at the edge of the ravine. Mute could make out the conversation. One was adamant he had heard something, but the other two weren't sure. The one wanted to find a way down to see.

Lia unconsciously moaned.

Softly, but distinctly.

Mute's hand shot to her mouth, capturing the sound. His head swiveled to capture her gaze when she opened her eyes, to mentally order her into silence. Nevertheless, her eyes remained closed. He

kept the bulk of his weight off her, but allowed
enough of it to pin her in case she started to move.
Keeping her quiet was imperative. He had no desire
to kill these men.

Rocks trickled, skittering down the slope to
land far too close for comfort. The insistent local was
searching for a way down. Mute held his breath, his
attention focused on the trio when Lia's head turned
under his palm. His gaze shifted to her, even though
his focus remained on the threat from above.

Amber eyes bore into his, darkening into burnt
gold even as they burned with white hot fury. Lia
hadn't moved, but those eyes told him all he needed
to know. His captive was gauging their present
situation while remembering the reason time, between
now and her last conscious thought, had been lost.

The men above prattled on impatiently. Mute
knew it was only a matter of seconds before the
persistent one plummeted to their level. Picking up a
hefty stone, aware the men weren't looking in the
right direction, he chunked it high, arching it toward
the west. It landed hard, clanking and starting a
cacophony of clatter only a small avalanche could
achieve. Mute almost closed his eyes in relief when
all three of the men moved in that direction a second
later. That minuscule reprieve seemed monumental.
The breath he'd been holding seeped out in a long,
slow sigh.

Under him, the stiffening of his prisoner
caught his attention. Lia had fully awakened. His
large hand on her mouth covered most of her face, but
her rounding eyes conveyed a lifetime of abhorrence
as they furiously glared into his.

The fire in those eyes seared him. Burned him deep. The accusation in them taunted him. Haunted him. They were accusing, distrustful, enraged---he could go on and on, for Lia's eyes promised a world of passion in them.

And he inwardly recoiled from the force, for absolutely none of it was pleasant. Still, the primary threat of discovery retreated and his body sagged in relief.

As if his relaxation triggered awareness and his prisoner realized her only hope of escaping was rapidly scurrying away, she writhed under him. Her muffled screams for escape slammed into his sweaty palm. Her body bucked, trying to throw him off. Slowly the anger in those huge eyes turned to fear, and she heaved and pitched, trying to dislodge him. All while shouting at the top of her lungs against his hot, heavy hand. The movements eventually lessened as a sad acceptance filled her shrinking body. Lia eventually stilled, her eyes condemning him to a slow, agonizingly painful death.

Mute remained motionless. Aware. Aware when the men left the area. Aware when it was safe. Still, he waited. Another few minutes passed in silence as Mute made sure the men resumed their original path. He ignored every feeble attempt Lia made to displace him from her torso. Finally, he felt safe enough to move. Still listening, Mute did a one-handed push up and eased off Lia. He was somewhat amazed at the quickness with which she skirted out from under him.

Lia abruptly back peddled on her knees, away from her captor. Her restrained hands clipped her pace, but her agility and speed surprised him. Huddling far back under the alcove of overhanging rocks, she drilled him with deadly intent in those dark amber eyes. Mute found himself suddenly wanting to discredit her fears.

That startled him.

"You hit me!"

Lia's words stung him. And, surprisingly, not from the vehemence in them.

He suddenly wished he hadn't.

What was wrong with him? It had never bothered him before to use a little force to gain a package's cooperation. Yet, something in him felt the need to explain. "For your own good."

Lia's head cocked to one side, reproach all too vivid. "No one was around. You hit me because I demanded an answer." Her tone had grown quiet, somber. One delicate eyebrow arched as both eyes narrowed. There was breathless disbelief in her tone as well. Incredulity replaced the resentment in her eyes. "I can't believe you did that." And then rage and contention filled those golden depths. "It's never okay to hit a woman. Real men don't hit women." Her chest rose sharply and then fell. There was finality in her voice. "Regardless."

Mute had no answer. No comeback. The accusation hit home. Suddenly, he felt obligated to justify his action. "Just a little tap. Nothing damaging." Previously inconceivable, the concept of defending himself made his voice harsh.

Lia mocked, her lips curling slyly. "A little tap. Nothing damaging." Those gorgeous eyes scalded every inch of him. "Just because I disagreed."

Full lips frowned as she again shot him a look that could and would kill the young, old, or frail. "I'd love to see what you do if…" sneering, she corrected, "*When* I disobey a direct order." The words were so short and sharp, they punched the air.

Mute cocked a thick eyebrow as a scowl settled on his face, his deep tone harsh, absolutely convincing. "No. You don't." The tight lines of his body removed any doubt. But when Lia's chin rose in defiance, he felt a sense of reluctant pride for the woman. A slight wariness masquerading real fear had crept into her eyes, revealing a tiny chink in her armor. But that square set of dainty shoulders matched the challenge of her lifted chin and low and behold, Mute couldn't help but admire the grit in this one, however stupid.

Or futile.

But grit wasn't something he had time to tolerate. He cocked his head, listening again to their surroundings. Satisfied they were once more alone, he curled strong fingers around her slender arm and pulled her up. "Time to move, Cinderella." He didn't wait for an answer, just pushed her in the right direction.

Lia stunned him by complying without even a disapproving glance. They moved along the ravine for Mute couldn't find a way up. And as they were heading in the correct direction he welcomed the benefits of invisible travel.

A couple of times Lia stumbled on the rocky and uneven terrain. Even a goat would have a hard time finding sure footing. As mere humans, they were subject to tripping, slipping, and even worse, ankle spraining falls. However, Lia never uttered a complaint. After a while Mute quit shoving at her shoulder when she slowed. They were making decent time, although not setting any records. He had to give her credit. Her feet proved as nimble as her body promised.

Mute strove to push that thought from his mind, but every so often an errant gust of wind would lift her blanket shirt, revealing tantalizing feminine details. Lean ribs encased in soft, creamy skin. A hint of rounded breasts. A smooth flat abdomen tapering into curved hips.

That latest shove he'd given her had been rougher than necessary, and he knew it.

Couldn't help it, but he knew it. Instead of the appropriate apology, he barked a loud command, "Move! We need to pick up the pace."

"Why? So I can die faster?" Lia's voice was faintly desperate.

Mute studied her back as she resumed her onward march. She was still ramrod straight, and each step was decisively placed. He felt a slight twinge about their purpose and wondered why. But he didn't speak, only kept them moving.

He was caught off guard when Lia suddenly stopped and spun, almost knocking him down.

Ice dripped from her tongue. "Oh Yeah?"

Mute mentally back pedaled to figure out what she was talking about. Then, and only then, was he able to understand she wanted assurance her death wasn't foremost on the agenda.

"If killing you was the objective...." He knew she understood his unspoken implication. She would be dead already if that was what his employer wanted. "DuPries wants that file."

Her eyes rounded with incredulity. "And you believe that?"

Mute was surprised he wanted to answer. But he clamped his mouth shut, refusing. It wasn't hard. Years of practice made it easy. Besides, a casual lift of one broad shoulder answered for him.

Her voice was so tinged with cynicism, it spat at him. "And you found the *quote unquote* stolen file on me or my person?"

He felt his eyes narrow at her question and the sarcasm. Still, he said nothing.

"Yeah. I guess one might go to great lengths to hide it if he had stolen something," Lia said. The mockery in her tone proved she was aware of his disbelief.

"She." His voice was hard. Iron hard. His eyes widened slightly when he realized he had responded, out loud.

The steel in her gaze matched his. And then those amber eyes flashed like lightning. "I didn't steal anything." She hurried on as if this was her last-ditch effort for salvation. "Since I didn't steal anything, I have to question the motive behind my kidnapping. Why would this Monsieur DuPries want me? Why would anyone?" Her defiant tone prompted a primal response from his gut. One he chose to ignore.

One darkly expressive eyebrow arched. But he remained silent. It wasn't his job to determine guilt, only to bring in his package. He knew his face remained impassive, but when a tangible flare struck in those amber eyes, he realized silence was also an accusation.

Lia glowered at him. But she didn't rise to the bait. "I've been trying to come up with any reason. Any excuse why someone would lie about me. Or want me. But there's none." Holding his gaze, she embellished, slowly and distinctly pronouncing every word. "I honestly have no idea why anyone on this entire planet would want me."

Mute didn't try to stop the wary glance he threw her. Too many guilty-as-hell proclaimed innocents had hardened him.

"I told you I don't know any DuPries." Her voice rasped with barely controlled anger.

He shrugged, backing up the fact he was only indulging in this tête-à-tête to relieve the boredom.

"I think the real question is…" Lia hesitated, as if testing a theory. "Who would gain by my absence?"

Mute let the silence lengthen, intent on remaining neutral. It drawled on as he watched the cogwheels in Lia's brain churn. He could almost see those neurons firing. Wonder hit hard when he realized he had answered her question with one of his own, out loud and verbally. "Who?"

"I wish I knew." Her eyebrows pinched together, knotting. Her gaze rested far in the distance and it was obvious the view wasn't registering.

He let out a skeptical sigh. Uncharacteristically, he said exactly what he was thinking. "Sure. I suppose you're neck deep in espionage, and certain Middle East countries have bounties on you."

"Of Course *Not*." Lia blew a loud breath out as if his cynicism was intolerable. "Contrary to popular belief, I am but a humble relief worker."

Mute remained silent, allowing his glare to speak for him. It must have worked too well for Lia drew in a sharp breath, her eyes shouting righteous indignity into his very soul.

"In Turkey. Sirmac, to be precise. Close enough to help the refugees from across the borders." Veracity replaced fury as she glared at him. "I spend my days delivering antibiotics, food, and threadbare rags to anyone brave enough to cross the border."

When her eyes unlocked his, he realized his expression must have leaned toward agnosticism. But he did nothing to dispute the obvious, remaining non-committal even though it crossed his mind to question why his employer would go to such great lengths to attain a commonplace Good Samaritan.

"I have no idea." It was as if she read his mind even though she had again focused on the perilous footing.

Mute made sure he kept his mouth shut. Not that it mattered. Von Stratham was thinking out loud and apparently on a roll.

"Unless the antibiotics were some kind of drug the government was keeping secret from the public? Or I treated someone wanted by the government? Or enemies of the government and I can identify them?" She let out a short breath. "Or maybe I overheard something or someone thought I did?" Her footsteps slowed as she warmed to the subject. "I don't know. Maybe I talked with a rebel leader in the infirmary? Maybe... I unknowingly passed on secret

documents thinking they were medical records?
Maybe I treated someone's worst enemy, and they
lived? Maybe I saw the wrong people and can
identify them? Maybe I was in the wrong place at the
right time? Maybe I…"

"Enough." Mute couldn't make sense of her
ramblings. Some were plausible. Even possible.
"Back up. You said you think the government was
allowing you to give out narcotics?" He didn't ask
himself why he was indulging her speculation.

"I don't know? How could I?" She sighed.
"The vials were labeled antibiotics. Normal
antibiotics. Penicillin. Amoxicillin. You know.
Antibiotics." Disbelieving eyes drilled deep even
though her glance was short and quick.

"So why wouldn't the government want you
to hand out medicine?" Even though the question was
an oxymoron, he let it stand.

Lia halted, appearing to puzzle over his
question for a moment. Not to mention, the fact he'd
actually spoken a full sentence. She shook her head as
if to clear it before she continued. "Of… of course…
the government allows medicinal help for its people."
Strength leaped into her voice. "But what if they were
conducting an experiment using God knows what on
unsuspecting people?"

He didn't answer.

Surprise. Surprise.

After a long pause, Lia finally admitted, "It
doesn't sound possible, does it?" Silence filled long
minutes. And then she stopped abruptly, turning
toward him, fastening him with damn near drown-
able depths of gold-flecked amber uncertainty.

Mute could only stare into that cosmic abyss, fully aware he was sinking. For a moment every cell in him, mind as well as body, burst with responsiveness. He felt the heat of it in every pore.

Before tamping it down.

The monumental effort produced a low snarl from pursed lips as he fought to retain his senses. He barely heard her next question.

"Does it?" Lia's voice wavered slightly. Sincerity softened the obstinacy of her chin, even the defiance in her eyes. She searched his, almost pleadingly.

Time stretched as her steadfast gaze pinned him to his very core.

She honestly expected him to answer.

For a split second, Mute wanted to give her exactly what she wanted. Fortunately, he found one of his inner rocks and managed to casually shrug one broad shoulder while muttering, "Nope." Hopefully, he was the only one who caught how ragged his voice sounded.

A rush of exhaled breath deflated a suddenly distraught Lia. Abruptly, she threw her head so far back it almost landed on her shoulder blades. So much so, her neck looked broken. Her eyes shut, tightening fiercely as she grimaced. Without warning, Lia opened her eyes and then screamed.

"Yahhh…." Torment focused her cry into something between a plea and a sob. Whatever it was, the sound was loud enough to be heard in the next country.

Mute rushed to her side, his hand clasping over her mouth with an iron grip. His own dark gaze contained real steel as he silently commanded her to be quiet.

She ignored his unspoken order and continued to yell. Slowly she brought her head level, pinning him with a relentless stare even as she continued to cry against his palm. Her body strained to pull away from his hand. Her eyes glistened with an anger that burned away the chance of tears, had any threatened.

Still, her abrupt acceptance of her circumstances combined with that obviously obstinate denial pulled something from his hardened soul. Mute suddenly wanted to pull her into his chest, wrap his arms around her and comfort the hell out of her.

What the hell?

He fought that insanity. The effort made his voice rough.

And his hands rougher. He tightened his grip on her mouth, leaning into her space as he menaced above her, growling a low warning. "Hush." Everything about him, from the glint in his dark eyes to the tips of his tense toes, promised the silent *Or else*.

Lia's eyes hardened, but she quieted. Still, her body remained tight as strung cable.

Mute didn't remove his hand for he didn't trust her to remain quiet. He kept his ears open for any response wrought from the sudden announcement of their position. Her breathing was ragged, little gasps as she struggled to breathe under his hand, but still, he didn't lift it. He scanned the area, searching for movement, listening for sound.

There was none, nor any change indicating an unseen presence. Mute relaxed his hand, but only enough to allow a little air to sift through his fingers. He turned to Lia, the hard planes of his face sharpening, as did his voice. The words were low, ringing with absolute promise. "No sound." His eyes narrowed to almost nothing. The harsh words ground out from behind a clenched jaw. "Got that?"

His hand bobbed as Lia hesitantly nodded. Her eyes still held a bucket full of defiance, but he could feel the tremor in her chin. Carefully he lifted his hand, ready to plop it back in place if she so much as uttered a loud breath.

She glared at him with a sixty-forty mixture of rage and despair. Hesitating, he lowered his hand to his side. Mute understood her scream was a reaction to the futility of the situation. A part of him wanted to promise it was going to get better.

That made him start. His teeth grated, making the words tight and angry. "Move. You're costing daylight." He gave her shoulder a hard shove, far more than was necessary.

One Lia wasn't ready for. It threw her off balance and she fell, landing on one knee, her torso tilting forward oddly. Hands tied behind her back created havoc with equilibrium. She gasped. Her body stiffened with the attempt to slow her forward momentum. Mute reached to grab her, but his hand caught only air. Lia hit the ground hard. Her eyes closed with the effort it took to contain a stifled groan of pain. He knew the depth of it, for her face filled with all she verbally held back.

Time seemed to stop.

Suddenly, her tawny eyes opened and attacked his with such vehemence Mute knew the blaze in her glare could start a fire in a bucket of water. Her face contorted with more fury than pain. Her lips flattened into a snarl. "Does it make you feel more of a man to attack defenseless women? Do you feel big and strong? Do you feel like a man now?" She made no attempt to get up. The wrath in her eyes could have started another world war. And then, somehow, that stare went nuclear. "Do you?"

Mute didn't allow the sympathy he felt to make even the slightest appearance. He kept his features granite hard, controlled. He reached for her blanket shirt, grabbing the front of it and forcefully hauled her to her feet, well aware of just how forceful when her feet thudded loudly as they again landed, after being lifted completely off the ground. Sometimes it was difficult to control all that brute strength.

But he forgot about that little slip quickly enough for he could feel the beginning swell of her breasts under his fist. He could feel the pounding of her heart for it was thumping wildly. He didn't immediately let go, for two reasons. One, to make sure she was steady on her feet. The other, his hand liked where it was.

Lia's wide eyes narrowed. She must have heard his quick intake of breath. Her tone filled with revulsion. "Real men don't manhandle women." She was leaning back, trying to ease from his grip. Her eyes held a terror she couldn't hide, even though her outthrust chin denied the fear.

Mute let go. He studied the scared woman before him. Lia's taunt was full bravado and he knew it. He'd felt the tremor. He smelled her fear.

It repulsed him, almost as much as the guilt swamping him.

He'd finally figured it out. It had taken time, for he was unaccustomed to either sentiment, especially the guilt. And he wasn't sure why he was feeling it now. After all, she was only his prisoner. Not his woman. His lower brain swelled even before he could finish the thought. He tamped down the raw desire flooding him.

Mute scrubbed his face clean of emotion. He thought it best if he didn't touch her right now. And not only for her benefit. A touch of mockery stamped his tone when he politely asked, "If you would be so kind to…" the request became an order. "Move."

Lia's eyebrows knotted for a moment before her face smoothed. She didn't answer but complied.

Once again, they were moving in the right direction.

Silence became the norm as they covered ground. Heat relentlessly baked the pair. Mute used what little shade was available when they rested or took a water break. Neither of which was frequent or long enough. Sweat beaded on every inch of his body and trickled down any crevice it could find. He knew on Lia's as well. Her hairline was dark and damp from perspiration. She didn't complain but, dammit, the blanket shirt was hot, too hot for this climate. But what choice did he have?

Mute pushed onward, resigned to not like anything about today.

Late in the afternoon, he found a partial cave and headed Lia into it. She needed to rest. She looked like the walking dead. He guessed the woman was accustomed to harsh conditions, but nothing like this. This trek through the desert would break seasoned locals.

Instinctively he knew he had pushed too hard, for Lia instantly collapsed when he gently pushed her down into a sitting position. She surprised him by abruptly crumpling, lying flat on her bound hands, hands that had to be acutely stabbing into her back. Her lackluster eyes closed. Her breathing was loud, coming in short ragged gasps as if she had just finished a marathon.

Shifting the pack off his back, he dug for water. He tapped her shoulder so she would rise and drink, but Lia never opened her eyes, much less moved. Instead, a vicious frown crossed her lower face as she threw out a question, impatience screaming in every syllable. "What do you want now?"

Mute grasped the front of her top and yanked her into a sitting position, thrusting a water bottle in front of her lips. When her mouth opened, he tilted the bottle up and carefully poured. Lia drank greedily, her mouth following the container when he pulled it away.

But her eyes never opened. Her body then resumed a reclining position, but her breathing seemed easier. Her expression appeared less fatigued, more restful, now her thirst had been partially quenched.

Mute took a quick swig and recapped the bottle. He studied his companion. Lia's hair was tangled and damp with sweat, two shades darker now. Exhaustion and travel dust had etched fine lines above the bridge of her straight nose as well as parenthesis around the edges of her lips. Tension had straightened her delicately arched eyebrows. Full lips had thinned as well. He was glad she was taking advantage of their brief respite and not starting another argument.

Before he could stop himself, he found himself gently rolling her over. Although his lips remained flat and tight, he almost felt the humor a smile would have produced as he observed how her eyes had flown open at the abrupt movement.

Or was it his touch? And then they widened moon big when he unsheathed the thick bladed knife from a side clip. Her body tensed, readied to scramble, but before she could move, he slipped the blade between her hands and cut the leather binding them. Lia's mouth flopped open, even though her hands remained behind her as if still imprisoned.

Mute never took his eyes off hers, knowing he would see any attempt to escape in her eyes long before she tried anything. When she made no effort to move at all, he pulled her arms forward.

Lia slowly sank until she was again lying on her back. Her eyes closed again. This time very tightly. Her face pinched as if she was fighting some huge cavern of emotion, maybe even tears. The tension in her face silently screamed a scrambled message of hope and frustration, even relief.

When she didn't move her arms or hands, Mute picked up the closest and began to lightly knead the feeling back into it, ignoring her soft gasp. Then he did the same to the other. By the time he had finished, Lia was rubbing long fingers over her bandaged wrists, not only to coax the blood back into them, but also to inspect the damage. She held up her hands, watching while wiggling her fingers as if fully aware she might never be able to again. Abruptly, she turned to him. "Thank you." Her voice was soft, completely sincere.

Mute didn't acknowledge her gratitude. He understood it, but remained silent.

Lia flexed her fingers, then her wrists, and then her arms. Sighing deeply, she closed her eyes again, seemingly to catch what little rest she could.

Mute pulled a t-shirt out of his duffle and threw it at Lia's drowsy form. He realized, too late, a warning would have been welcome. She jerked, eyes fluttering open, startled by the sudden assailment. Her voice sounded rusty. "What's this for?" She picked up the t-shirt, staring at it, and then at him, and then again at the shirt.

"Put it on." Mute kept his tone neutral.

"Huh?" Lia looked puzzled.

"It will be cooler than that blanket."

Lia's eyes narrowed. "Okayyy..." She let the last syllable drag, landing a half-octave up. "And you get to watch." It wasn't a question, and they both knew it.

"Turn around." Mute had no intention of falling for an escape attempt.

Lia impaled him with a glare before sitting up. She continued to stare at him for a long minute before she pulled up her knees and then rotated until he was staring at her back. An utterly feminine back, with delicately carved shoulders and blades tapering subtly to a narrow waist. All covered in velvety soft skin.

Lia tugged the coarse blanket up and over her head shakily, for her arms were stiff and inflexible. Quickly, Lia pulled on the t-shirt. She remained turned as she smoothed the fabric. Still another moment passed before she twisted around.

Her eyes were questioning, but her voice softened. "Thank you." She was studying him. "Again."

Mute didn't even nod. He openly stared at her, heat filling his eyes. He couldn't help it. Even dirt stained and covered in sweat, she was beautiful.

Need filled him.

Want hit him like a car crash.

Sudden.

Merciless. A wallop of desire consumed him. Mute gritted his teeth until his jaw hurt, fighting the fire heating his blood. Every muscle in his body tensed. He couldn't look away. Duty went blood deep.

Mute forced an image of the payoff to the surface. When that didn't tamp down the desire, he thought about the details of this assignment and the accusations against Lia. Still, it was only when he began to recite the Gettysburg address in his head that the heat lessened. By then, Lia had once more resumed nap position, her now free hands lying weightlessly on her stomach, eyes shutting out the world.

And him.

Mute's gaze wandered over her, finally landing on the tiny mole above her lip. Damn, that was sexy as hell. He forced himself to look away.

Concentrating on the objective, he decided a thirty-minute nap would do them both good. There had been no sign of anyone in the area recently so he felt reasonably confident they were alone. His only problem, at the moment, was if his captive chose to use this respite to escape.

Mute noiselessly slid to Lia's side and eased her hands together to lie on her belly. He swiftly retied them before fastening the loose end to his left wrist. He lay down beside her and closed his eyes. Listening to the silence, he could hear how steady Lia's breathing was. He turned, studying her. Her mouth was slightly open, and her face remained relaxed.

Exhaustion had won. She was already asleep. It took every bit of control not to caress her rumpled hair, her cheek, or let his thumb trace the outline of her sensuous mouth. Mute closed his eyes, willing his body to ignore the need this woman aroused in him.

Mute slept lightly, but sleep he did.

He awoke to a tentative movement tugging on his arm. Without opening his eyes, he knew his captive was trying to extricate herself. A smile would have crossed his lips if he was the sort, but since he wasn't, his face remained impassive.

He let Lia attempt her escape. She occasionally let out a barely audible grunt every so often, usually accompanied by a gentle tug on his wrist.

Just when he felt the cord at his wrist give way, he spoke, his voice the only sign he was awake. And alert. It was deadly soft. "And where would you go?" Mute opened his eyes, capturing hers.

Lia's shocked expression was adorable. Incredulity stamped her face as she stammered, "Uh... I... I didn't..." And then her face fell. For a moment, he thought she was going to burst into tears.

But they never materialized. Defeat surfaced and then dejection took over that gorgeous face. Her voice turned bland while her upper body slumped. Apparently, she found the ground fascinating. "Just... away."

It was best to explain her predicament. "Away will get you killed or worse." Mute's tone deepened. "If the heat doesn't kill you, or a wild animal, then the two-legged variety certainly will. If they don't rape and beat you before selling you to the first person with a few Liras."

Lia's eyes, wide as twin moons, involuntarily sought his. Her lips pressed together and thinned. "I don't believe you."

He shrugged.

Not his problem.

Lia thrust her chin up and stood. She gave him a hard glare, promising anywhere would be better than staying with him. She quickly struggled out of the remaining bindings, letting them fall to the ground in front of her. She leveled Mute with a determined glare for two long moments before she spun and started walking in the direction from which they had come.

Mute had to admire her courage, however ineffectual.

He let her go.

Until she was a good hundred feet away. After a cleansing sigh, he called after her. "Be careful not to disturb any locals. They don't respect women. Much less a woman traveling alone."

As expected, Lia pulled up short, her tiny gasp hung interminably.

Even he had to hand it to her. She straightened her shoulders, without turning or looking at him, and continued. Clearly, remaining with him wasn't her favorite option.

Mute sat up.

For a long time, he watched her trudge away and then let his head hang when it registered he would have to expend a fair amount of energy getting her back. This woman had no intention of making his mission easy or uncomplicated. A soft sigh escaped him.

But a tiny, almost invisible curl turned up the outer corner of his lips. He actually believed it did. In reality, only the left side lifted slightly.

Mute laboriously rose to his feet.

He didn't call to her, wanting to keep noise to a minimum and immediately covered the distance between them within seconds. Wrapping strong fingers around her forearm, he pulled her up short. She landed hard against him, chest to chest. Haunting amber eyes held a tangible question. The one asking if she was better off without him, or with him.

For a long, long moment.

And then the alarm in those eyes hardened into purpose as Lia brought up her right arm, the glint of a blade momentarily blinding him as her hand slashed down toward his chest.

Mute barely sidestepped in time. His mouth hanging open had tripped up his timing. And then he had to dodge several attempts on his person as Lia thrust and swung his very own knife, trying to injure him or even hasten his untimely demise.

He sidestepped easily and ducked when necessary. Silently, and without striking back, he allowed her to tire. She would find fatigue a formidable enemy, and he knew it. He hadn't made it easy on her. Trussed up the previous night without rest and then a full day in this relentless, life-sucking heat had taken its toll. Although the attack alone was knight-worthy valiant, it had only taken a dozen or more attempts on his life for Lia to finally grasp she was outclassed, not only in brawn, but in brains, when it came to hand-to-hand combat.

Not to mention, just too damn tired.

Mute almost wished he had let her get a decent wound into him when she abruptly chunked the knife at him, handle first, while yelling a soft, dejected cry at her ineptitude.

Hoarsely she screamed at him. "Just go ahead and kill me." She threw him a shattered plea. "Now. Just do it. Get it over with." Her eyelids clamped tight as if she was shutting off sudden water works. But when she abruptly opened them, for no move had been made against her, Mute knew, with absolute certainty, tears weren't on the agenda.

Rage was.

Exhaustion was.

Acceptance was.

Resignation.

She'd grasp she was no longer in control. Her freedom was gone, completely ripped away. It would be the ultimate humiliation for someone like her, for the very idea of captivity was inconceivable for anyone who could claim such an innocent background.

Mute swallowed hard, but he didn't let his body relax as he bent to pick up his knife. Damn, he had to admire this one. She had stolen his own weapon and used it against him. His lips remained in their customary frown, but he thought they were lifting at the corners. He really did.

Solemnly his gaze consumed his prisoner as he sheathed the knife. Whether it was intentional or not, his stance towered over her resigned form. Mute was very aware of her submission, not only to his brute power but to her circumstances. What made him marvel was her ability to acknowledge the inevitable.

While not accepting the foreseeable.

For there remained a very tangible *for now* in her present surrender.

It was at that precise moment his lips lifted for the first time in years. Both corners, actually quirking up.

And Mute didn't even realize it.

Without a word, he spun her roughly, dragging her hands behind her back and trussed her up like a Thanksgiving turkey. He didn't want to dodge any more attempts on his life by her hand, however incompetent. He gave her a hard push, intent on returning for the backpacks. Her expression only hardened when he situated his into its proper place before refastening hers onto her back. His unspoken order to continue was in his insolently lifted lone eyebrow. Lia threw him a furious glance as if she could kill him with the arrows shooting from her eyes, before following his silent command.

Their journey continued along the gorge concealing their presence.

They walked for hours. Steady.

And silent.

Dusk was painting the sky peachy purple when Mute heard a strange, gargling sound. He stopped abruptly to listen. When Lia kept going, he thrust out a huge hand and tugged on the strap of her backpack. She halted, turning exasperated eyes to his.

"What now?" Her voice was caustic. Exhaustion had taken its toll. Her expression shouted disinterest.

Mute wanted total silence to gauge the sound. When he finally got it, he wished he hadn't. Recognizing the suddenly swelling sound, the hiss, along with the growing roar, he scoured the gully they had been following the better part of the day for an escape route.

He found none.

There was no way up.

No way out.

Five

Mute let out a low, sharp curse as he frantically sought an escape.

The roar became insistent. And louder. He started running, dragging Lia with him. She opened her mouth to question, but never got the opportunity. Unexpectedly, she was running full out beside him, her eyes wild. He dropped his hand from her arm for she was suddenly ahead of him, out-distancing him.

Mute spotted a lone spike of a dead tree ahead and made a beeline for it, pulling Lia to a stop alongside him. His eyes signaled hers, yelling silently for cooperation even as he pulled out the very knife she had tried to kill him with and cut her loose. Using her restraints, he tied them both to the tree and silently prayed the roots ran deep.

Lia's eyes rounded and then widened beyond belief at his own imprisonment with her, but Mute never had the opportunity to explain, to tell her what was coming.

For just then the rushing wall of water flooding the ravine was upon them. The angry, frothing, dirty grey wall of the devil's own flash flood stretched out like Lucifer's fingers as it carried everything in its path to Hell and beyond, with Mute and Lia caught smack in the middle of its destructive path.

Mute barely had time to wrap his arms around her, clamping her close. He ordered harshly, "Take a deep breath," and then led by example. Before the weight of the flood wall hit them, he was able to grab the waistline of her pants into his grip as well as her T-shirt. He willed his arms to hold tight and secure.

Mute took a giant breath and braced.

The flood hit them with the force of a runaway train. He had never experienced the feeling of his skin trying to rip from his body, but this was his first flash flood.

Focusing strength into his arms and legs, he fought, digging his feet into the softening ground as he forced his legs to remain steadfast and true. Water swirled furiously past him, threatening to drag them down and away. His eyes closed as he took the brunt of the surging wave, shielding his prisoner with his body, his strong arms wrapping her completely within his grip as well as the bending tree. His mouth snarled as he fought the brute force of its angry, mad rage, allowing a tiny seepage of moisture in. A welcome wetness after burning in the desert all day, although one Mute never had time to enjoy.

He hung on, willing his fingers to cling to her. To hang on for dear life for he knew if he lost his grip, Lia would drown. There wasn't a man alive who could out-swim a raging, violent flash flood, much less one of this magnitude. And Lia was already exhausted beyond limit.

Mute concentrated on his fingers, the hands keeping her within his grip. His mind shut out the hits to his body from the debris the river swept along its destructive path. Along with the fact his chest was starting to swell with need for oxygen, but the water was still too high, too deep. He refused to think about oxygen, all the while praying Lia had gotten enough in her lungs to ride this out.

Miraculously, the water began a delicate calming, the debris field clearing somewhat. His body wasn't being pummeled as before. Although they were still under water, Mute knew the flash of the flood was over. The rage of it had passed them. All that was left was the torturous path of rapids and debris.

Only when Lia began to kick wildly with her feet, her arms flailing, did Mute move. And then only his eyelids. They opened, surveying the aftermath, thankful he was still breathing.

As was Lia.

The flood had been as brief as it was violent. The worst was over. The water receded quickly as most of the volume followed the path of the gulch.

Mute was still clutching at her clothes with his right hand even as his left arm was still wrapped around the tree with Lia in between. Realization flooded him with the same force of the actual flood and he let go, retreating. Automatically, he cut the binding holding them to their lifeline of support. Backing away, he tamped down the adrenaline singing through his veins. He spit, trying to rid himself of the steely taste of destruction from the raging waters, of the deluge that had threatened their very existence.

Lia stood in front of him, bent at the waist, retching water from her mouth and nose. Mute had swallowed more than he had needed as well and followed suit. When the retching stopped, the gagging began. And then the gasping for breath.

Only Mute kept his gasps to a minimum. For it was then he understood the damage he had sustained.

One or more ribs had been broken.

Or badly bruised. Left side.

Most likely from the mine field of debris swept along with the raging waters. But knowing the cause didn't heal the injury. Mute took short breaths, adjusting to the pain. It wasn't the first time. Nor would it be the last.

The water had lessoned to a trickle. He surveyed the damage to his prisoner. She was doubled over, struggling to expel the water she had inadvertently swallowed.

Lia retched. Coughed. Sputtered. And then cursed unabashedly as waves of nausea hit. Dry heaves wracked her slim shoulders. Her body protested violently against the torture of nearly drowning, and then began trembling with shock. Yet when her glare captured his gaze, it was obvious her temper flamed white hot for having to endure yet another torture.

Mute forgot his pain as hers crept all through him. He had to admire the guts it took for her to shake off the queasiness and nausea to face him with such vehemence. Lia had coughed up the equivalent of a small pond. Apparently, she hadn't understood the order to take a deep breath.

Of oxygen.

He remained perfectly still as her eyes threatened to set him on fire. Or shoot daggers into him. Or torture him a thousand ways, with death his only release. Still, it wasn't only the threat in her eyes that held him immobile, but the sharpness of his ribs. Shoving the pain down to a manageable level, he waited for her to vocalize her complaint.

The wait vanished. "And just how… did you manage… to convince Mother Nature… to join you in your cause?" The words struggled out, her voice ragged, but furious.

Mute didn't answer. The question was insipid.

Lia ranted further. "You must tell me your secret. I've never known anyone who could command nature." Her upper lip curled into a defiant snarl.

Mute drank in a deep breath, ignoring the pain, as he stood against her vehemence.

It was then he recognized her body was shaking, shivering violently, and it wasn't from their narrow escape from death.

The truth suddenly hit him. She was cold. Freezing.

As was he.

No wonder.

Night had fallen and every ounce of heat from the day had vanished. Exponentially compounding the cold from the dousing they had endured.

He spun into action. Quickly, his eyes searched their surroundings, finding what he needed. A small fingerling off the ravine, situated meters higher than the crevice that had concealed them for most of the day. And even better, above the water-line the leftover flow of water had created.

Mute dragged Lia along, not answering her abrupt, "Hey…" He lifted her bodily into the fissure before attacking the next problem.

Shelter. And warmth.

Furiously he worked, finding ample materials from the resulting cacophony the flash flood had delivered. Gathering driftwood and fallen limbs, he shoved them into position above head level, driving the larger branches deep into the soft earth as he weaved a leafy roof overhead. The smaller ones would be used for kindling. He knew better than most how dangerous hyperthermia could be.

Working swiftly, he laid tender into a small pattern well below the canopy of branches. Carefully he ignited an emergency match. Blowing softly, he established a small fire, fully aware the smoke would be minuscule, practically invisible by the time it swirled past the leaf-laden boughs of the roof he'd constructed. The risk of discovery was a calculated one. However, certain death from hypothermia outweighed detection.

At the moment.

He fed the flame slowly, letting each piece burn when it caught. It took time, but it was necessary. The fire would warm them both.

Mute's ribs protested, but he disregarded the pain and continued the task, knowing, at the very least, he was saving extremities, if not their very lives. The flames grew, starting to warm them, not only with heat but also with its visual presence.

He wasn't the only one trembling from the cold. He turned, finding Lia shivering uncontrollably. Without hesitation, he reached for her. A tiny portion of his brain was shocked she hadn't tried to escape. She was freed. Completely unrestrained, but when he locked his hands around her body, he understood.

Lia literally couldn't move. Trauma and temperature had rendered her immobile. Her body trembled violently from the cold. The chilling drop in temperature of the oncoming night only added to the numbing cold of her soaked clothes. Mute also knew the minute he stopped moving he, too, would succumb to the freezing paralysis as well.

He gave her no warning, suddenly pulling Lia close and roughly jerking her clothes off. Every stitch. Her face scrunched up to protest, but her mouth, although rounded, remained silent when she met the determination in his eyes. He then draped the dripping mess amidst the branches overhead.

Without preamble, he shucked out of his own. It was difficult to remove his T-shirt one-handed, and he struggled. A low groan hissed through clenched lips before he abandoned the effort and concentrated on his pants. Like most with his background, commando was the norm, so he didn't have to deal with nonessentials like underwear.

Suddenly he felt his shirt being tugged up.

Mute's head dropped as he probed Lia's eyes. His eyebrows rose a micro millimeter as his gaze scanned a blushing, but resolved Lia. Purpose had won over embarrassment. Apparently, she too, had come to the realization they would freeze to death long before their clothes dried on their own. Tugging his shirt fully up and over his head, she grimaced. It had to be hard to stretch that far when her arms must be achy and stiff from being tied behind her back all day. She met his eyes directly as she handed the shirt to him.

Mute didn't allow the gratitude to touch his expression, but it hit hard.

Not something he was used to. And for some unknown reason, the knowledge she had volunteered help irritated him. It wasn't that he needed it, but the fact she had offered. A slow snarl began to gather in his throat. His clamped jaw wouldn't allow it to escape. Nor could the string of curses ranting through his brain make it past his clenched teeth. Without a word, he turned and using one arm, hung his clothes next to hers.

Six

Lia remained motionless.

Well, as still as her quaking body could. Her legs felt like jelly, but the thought of sitting on the ground, naked, turned her already queasy stomach. Her eyes grazed the area, searching for the least objectionable resting spot. Pebbles and rock littered the ground, cutting into her feet. She hated to think how it would feel on bare skin, along with the, yuck and double yuck, mud that would coat and cover her.

But the sight of the fire was comforting. Not that she could feel much. Lia looked up from the subtle red glow to find her captor gathering the biggest rocks. She studied him, wondering the reason, as he began to bank the largest along the ravine side of the fire. The fire alternately grew and receded, highlighting and then shadowing the muscles and sinewy shape of the man tending it. Lia was mesmerized, not only with his expertise but by the man himself.

Either completely immodest or unabashedly proud for damn good reason, he continued to work.

Lia finally concluded it was neither. The man had a job to do.

"Move to the other side of the fire." His terse order broke the silence and her concentration.

Lia jumped, startled. It was out of her mouth before she could stop it. "Why?"

His left eyebrow rose slightly, but Lia had seen that barely imperceptible movement before and retribution had been swift and harsh, each and every time. Now was no different.

She involuntarily cried out when his arm snaked toward her, pulling her opposite of the flames. And closer to him. His mouth clamped and a muscle jumped in his jaw.

Lia knew he hadn't spoken, but she could feel the words in her head as if he had shouted them, the actuality of them pounding against every recess in her mind.

Because I said so.

One question suddenly popped in her head, an incomprehensible question. A question only the man before her could answer. *Just how in the hell can one shout without uttering a single word?*

Her own eyes narrowed. She opened her mouth to tell him exactly what he could do with his orders but wasn't given time for the brute suddenly dropped to the ground, one arm clamping her tight against his length, dragging her down with him.

Lia fell on top of him. A soft *humph* expelled what little breath she had managed to hoard. Falling into the hardness of solid muscle and hot skin, Lia instantly lost what little remaining oxygen her lungs had hidden. Her lips, as well as the rest of her, were suddenly plastered against the breadth and width of him. It took her a long moment to understand what he had done, much less where she had ended up.

His naked body under hers.

Lia tried desperately not to relish in the feel of skin on skin. Tawny gold eyes widened as she looked everywhere, but into his dark ones. Her mind raced, tumultuously so, as did the knowledge he wanted to spare her bodily injury when he had dropped onto the hard, jutting ground. His own absorbing enough for them both when he lay fully on his back. They both needed to rest and he had taken her inability to recline for what it was.

Reluctance. A complete unwillingness to accept the conditions she now faced. Dirt, rocks, and all.

Lia struggled against his grasp, backing away from the length of him, her eyes apologizing even as she fled. Still, she felt the need to express it verbally. "I'm sorry. I didn't mean to… I hadn't… I hope I didn't…" Lia's tongue tripped over itself. Her troubled gaze traveling over her companion, telepathically picking up the barest trace of humor he wasn't physically expressing, once more strictly an impression.

It only reminded her how inhuman and callous he was. She hissed out a loud breath as anger replaced the benevolence she had felt.

Was that only a moment ago?

And that anger flamed furiously when he grabbed her and pulled her on top of him.

Again.

His eyes bore into hers, but it was an empty stare. His voice held nothing more than explanation. "We both need the body heat."

Lia's body knew it. It was traitorously glorying in his warmth and everything else about him. Knowing he was right gave her the ability to manage a slight nod of acceptance. She stilled. Nonetheless, as hard as she tried, relaxation remained an impossible goal.

Knowing she had to didn't necessarily translate into able to.

It didn't help that all that wonderful, incredible heat beneath her, that velvet covered bronze, warmed her insides as well as her outside.

It took a very long time, but slowly, between gradually diminishing episodes of uncontrollable shivers, she began to warm. And then, relax. Exhaustion snuck up on her, and her eyelids grew heavy. She grudgingly allowed her head to lie in the hollow of his deliciously warm shoulder, permitting herself the pleasure of reveling in his warmth and masculinity.

Her hand reflexively crept up to rest beside her cheek as her breathing evened and slowed, inadvertently tweaking a masculine nipple as it traveled lightly up his chest.

Suddenly, Lia felt his masculinity press into her lower abdomen. All the warmth and pleasure, as well as that protective feeling, suddenly vanished. Her fantasy never included rape.

Panic filled her, and she pulled away, eyes wide with alarm. A long, hoarse plea sprang from her suddenly dry throat. "Please. Nooo…"

A solid and powerful arm tightened around the swell of her buttocks, his huge splayed hand clamping her tightly in place as Mute held her. An indiscernible look matched his conversational tone. "I don't do unwilling. Don't have to." Locked, clamped fingers surrounding the full swell of her hip loosened.

That powerful grip transformed into almost a tender embrace.

Lia couldn't help the explosion of her sigh. She hadn't known she'd been holding her breath. Nor was she convinced of her safety. Even with that so eloquent denial, his hard-on was still impressive. She couldn't escape his steely grip, but she remained wary and tense, ready to fight to the death if necessary. Her heart pounded in her chest. All thoughts of sleep had vanished.

She noticed he sucked in a quick, short breath when he lifted his left hand, before he gently pushed her head back down on his chest, his body relaxing slightly. Either, something was wrong with his torso for, although he hadn't uttered a sound, a faint flash had crossed his face when he had struggled to take off his T-shirt, or the man wanted quiet.

Lia couldn't be sure.

That flash could only be pain. Apparently, the man had been injured protecting her with his body during the flood. The knowledge allowed a tiny measure of calm to again settle the bulk of her terror.

Still, she remained tense, but as time passed without incident, she succumbed, again settling in the hollow of his chest. Her tension eased when she felt the length of him soften.

Although completely crazy, a small part of her bristled at his control. And that senseless, idiotic, stupid side refused to listen to reason as she warred within herself.

And subsequently lost.

Lia couldn't believe it was she who sank her body into his, moving suggestively as she settled into his length, intimately closer. Allowing herself the privilege of soaking up pure male perfection as her instantly taunt nipples toyed with his pecs. It was all she could do to smother the moan forming in the back of her throat at the feel of such masculinity. Clamping down the desire fighting within her seemed impossible.

And apparently it was, for the foolhardy and crazy part of Lia actually smothered a small grin when his desire was once more poking her in the belly.

Mute sucked in a short breath even as his hand abruptly jerked her chin up, his eyes narrowing as they locked with her suddenly innocent ones. From the look in his eyes, he wasn't deceived by their widening. Or the naivety Lia was desperately trying to pour from hers.

His voice was monotonous as if denying the intensity behind his question. "You willing?" His other hand was teasing the goose bumps suddenly covering her butt. In one swift move, he'd rolled her under him, pressing into her, grinding his entire length fully against her. Every ounce of him ready to accept anything she was willing to give.

The ground was sharp, cutting into her backside, but Lia wasn't aware. One hot hand was stealthily climbing up her hip, passing the curve of her waist, until it rested just under her breast, his thumb making lazy circles over her ribs. She grabbed a giant breath and silently cursed herself.

This was her fault, hers alone. "You're hurt." It wasn't a question. It was a statement that did exactly what it was meant to do. Change the subject, and, more importantly, the mood.

He studied her with a molten gaze and Lia couldn't breathe. Her lungs were burning for oxygen before the heat left his eyes and he turned away, rolling onto his back again.

Lia hurried on, afraid of not only his actions but her own reaction. "You're injured." Her eyebrows knotted when his dark inquiry turned from her.

He gave a slight shrug before again meeting her probing eyes, denial entirely evident in his exaggerated silence.

"You're lying." Lia tried to figure out a way to use this knowledge to her advantage. But she didn't even know where they were, much less how this would prove beneficial. Even worse, how to extract the heated stirrings this man had just elicited.

Mute just shrugged again, not bothering to deny her accusation. Languidly, he got to his feet and ran a hand over their clothes.

She tried not to stare, but what woman could resist the Adonis in front of her?

Apparently not her. Clamping her lips tight, and with every muscle tensing, she turned away, refusing to watch as he, one-handedly, retrieved their clothes. He threw her a T-shirt before pulling on his pants, and then donned his own shirt as well.

Lia picked up the now dry shirt and stood, wanting underwear and jeans. The jeans were still damp, but the rest was ready to wear. She was grateful and didn't waste any time getting dressed. She'd have to wait a little longer for the jeans, but just covering up was enough for the moment. She was smoothing the shirt over her hips when she looked up and found his dark eyes on her, his usual languid gaze absent. Still, she couldn't read his enigmatic expression.

Lia would've given real money to know what was going on in that brain of his. Swallowing hard, she was suddenly aware of how desperately she wanted to know. Wanted to know what he was thinking.

What was wrong with her? He was her captor, her enemy. His opinion shouldn't matter.

What she needed was to escape and for that, she needed to know his plans. Lia studied him.

Without looking directly into it, he fed the fire, the slight flame leaping hungrily at the small branches he offered it. The firelight played over his defined face, emphasizing the drawn lines and hardness of it. A man capable of anything, she thought. Anything and everything.

Lia considered him. She needed information, and he was her only option. Having already learned the ineffectiveness of hostility, a friendlier approach seemed wise. It wouldn't hurt to try. She cleared her throat and quietly asked, "Who are you?"

He didn't answer. Or even look up.

Lia felt her cheeks flush with heat. Her fists landed on her hips as she asked again. This time, her voice raised a couple decibels. "What's your name?"

Only then did he focus on her, his eyes studying her from under heavy lids. But he didn't speak.

"Good God. Don't you even have a name?" She let out an exasperated sigh before she began to ramble, furious with the man who didn't respect her enough to answer a simple question. "I don't know why I'm asking." Unconsciously, one hand sliced through the air. "Other than to avoid yelling *Hey you*." Clenched fists planted themselves on her hips. "But since you're so inept at conversation. I guess it doesn't even matter. Apparently, you take strong and silent to a whole new level. Well, I've got news for you. Talking is how normal people co-mu-ni-cate." Lia deliberately pronounced each syllable. "You can't do anything but issue orders, can you?"

She let out an explosive sigh. Her shoulders dropping as her frown deepened. Still, her eyes begged. "Okay, since you won't tell me your name, then tell me, how did this Monsieur Du…" Apparently anger had stolen parts of her memory. "Something contact you?"

Lia waited, but he only stared at her, eyes mere slits.

Suddenly desperate to know why she was living this particular nightmare, Lia stomped to his side. Using most of what little strength she had left, she punched his shoulder with a tight fist.

And then fought the desire to hop on one leg and yell *Ow*. Her hand throbbed with pain. It had been like hitting a steel pole. She couldn't help a small grimace as she faced her captor, holding her hand gingerly, absently flexing it. "Why won't you answer just one question? You… you… sorry, worthless, piece of…"

"Mute." His voice was toneless.

She stilled, her mouth gaping. "Huh?" She waited, speechless for once.

He was not and shrugged one shoulder eloquently.

She repeated his exclamation. "Mute." Her mouth rounded as her eyebrows knotted. "What does that mean? I don't understand. What does that have to do with meeting someone you call…"

He interrupted her, his jaw tightening. "You asked my name."

It took a moment, but Lia finally got it.

And before she could help it, laughter surfaced, bubbling out, enough she doubled over with it, laughing so hard tears slid down her cheeks. She could barely get the words out between deep guffaws. "Mute? Your name is Mute?" Her tone denied acceptance. She couldn't help but repeat the question. "Honest to God, your name is Mute?"

He didn't voice an answer. His unswerving gaze was ample reply.

Lia's giggling stilled to a manageable level. But she couldn't resist the jab. "Your mother named you Mute?"

"My C.O. did."

Lia's eyes brightened, brimming with curiosity. "What's a C.O.?"

Mute shrugged, this time with both shoulders. "Commanding Officer."

"You were in the military?" Lia surveyed her injured fingers, watching them open and close, making sure they still worked. Her hand really hurt from when she hit him. When Mute didn't answer, she jerked her head up, drilling him with a probing stare. "What branch of the military?" Her mouth rounded as a surreal thought slipped into her head. "We *Are* talking American military? Right?"

He nodded slightly. "Army." A penetrating hardness in his gaze contradicted an apathetic tone. "Rangers."

"You're a Ranger?" Her voice lowered with awe. Lia had only rudimentary knowledge of that official Bad Ass organization but was sufficiently impressed.

"Was." His indolent attitude implied this was strictly casual conversation, but she wasn't deceived.

"Were, uh, were you kicked out?"

His torso jerked only a minuscule amount, but Lia picked up on it. "Recruited," he corrected.

"Ah…" Lia breathed out the word, making it a long one for she still didn't understand. Glancing quickly at dark, knowing eyes, she realized her bluff was futile. So, she asked, "Recruited? By whom?"

His refusal to answer prompted another question.

"Why?" Delicate eyebrows knitted as she waited.

Mute didn't answer. He turned and then scrounged around in his duffle, pulling out a couple of MRE's. He glanced up at her, yelled an inaudible warning with a slight rising of one eyebrow before tossing her one.

Barely, just barely, Lia caught it.

He settled on the hard ground and then ripped the Meals, Ready-To-Eat open and began to chow down. She hesitated a moment longer, but when the silence stretched, she understood the conversation was over. Turning the silver packet over in her hand, she read the block letters, the contents of the meal.

Salisbury steak. Oh yeah, her favorite.

Lia looked up at him, noting he was still watching her, even as he ate. He may be under orders not to kill her but did those orders include keeping her fed. Did they include keeping her warm? As warm as when he'd clamped their bodies together for heat? When his body spoke of fulfilling more than warmth?

Sincerity filled her gentle tone. "Thank you." For the very first time, she got an abrupt sense of surprise from the man.

He stilled suddenly as his gaze bore into her. And then just as rapidly, he resumed consuming his meal, his expression bland. Or was there a touch of wariness in it?

Lia decided on no and opened her meal. After a few tentative bites, she chewed anyway. Her scowl was sufficient indication of what she thought about tonight's cuisine, but it had been over twenty-four hours since she had last eaten. Besides, after another few bites, she determined it wasn't that bad. It only tasted slightly of dried leaves and plastic. And when Lia found the bar of artificially flavored chocolate, mercy and oh my, she was in heaven.

Seven

"Grrr…" Mute finally permitted a verbal snarl to accompany the frown flattening his lips, allowing every bit of his pent-up frustration to growl up from the depths of his throat. His fingers tightened mercilessly around the totally indestructible, waterproof military-grade and completely shattered cell phone that was now utterly unusable. Pieces of plastic and wiring filled his palm.

And this worthless piece of shit was his backup.

Lia's gasp was audible, her rounding eyes almost erasing the exhaustion that had, over the last two days, enveloped and finally consumed her. Her voice was just as weary as her body. "So he talks." Disgust filled her slurred words.

Mute threw one of his signature vacant glances at her before resuming his task. Staring down at the disassembled bits and pieces of plastic and components, he ignored her, as he had for the last two days.

He knew what was coming. Lia would again shift into her one-sided conversation about where they were now, where they were going, who was Monsieur DuPries, and what seemed to be a hundred different scenarios of possible reasons why he was dragging her halfway across the barrens of Turkey to face someone she didn't know.

Oh Yeah. He knew exactly what was coming.

Occasionally she would also add *his* statements to her questioning commentary as well. Not that he would have actually said anything she made up.

Still, he had let her ramble. It hadn't interfered with his objective.

Mute focused on his present task. The piece-of-crap now cradled in his hand was the only link with his contact and as they were now over twenty-four hours overdue...

He went back to work.

Leveling the point of his knife at one particular connection on a tiny IC Chip, he held it in place and then pressed a button, listening.

Nothing. Dammit, nothing.

Lines of irritation creased his forehead. Only years of practiced patience kept him from crushing the tangle of wires and components into pulp.

"Well, technically that wasn't talking." Lia continued wearily. "But it was a sound." Her hand waved in the air, the gesture too haggard to properly indicate him. "If someone had told me a human being could go a full day without talking, I would never have believed them." Her shoulders bunched before dropping wearily as if it was too much effort. She let out a short, derisive snort. "Oh. I forgot." Amber eyes turned golden and then burnt gold as intolerance and anger filled them. Her voice seemed drained. "You're not human. So, you don't count. Do you?" She averted her whole body as if dismissing him, but her eyes never released his.

Mute stared down at the inoperable mess in his hand for a long time before he looked at her, his body flag-pole rigid.

"Do you?" Amber eyes taunted far more than words.

Mute was up and by her side in one single stride, his fingers digging into her biceps as he spun her to face him. Catching his infuriated reflection mirrored in her eyes, he inhaled deeply, striving for control. It was about as calming as dousing a fire with gasoline for he caught the scent of her on the air. And then on his tongue. His fury flamed. He drew her closer until her wide, suddenly terror-filled eyes were only a hair under his nose. An angry growl grew in the back of his throat, and although it wasn't deliberate, Mute didn't stop it. The whisper of it morphed into a strangled roar.

Lia tried to pull back and away. A whimper sounded from behind her trembling lips. Her chin began to quiver even though amber eyes remained dry, although instantaneously too bright and glistening for tears not to be threatening. "I'm sorry. I'm sorry." Breathlessly she repeated, "I'm sorry. I shouldn't have said that. You're…" Her words trailed off as if she didn't know what to say.

Mute answered for her, his voice deceptively low. "Completely human." Without hesitation, he crushed her lips with his own. Hard. Bruising. Exacting. His lips devoured hers, taking sweet revenge for the endured torture of her, of her presence. The agony of denying himself the slightest pleasure of just one touch. He forced his tongue between her tight lips and tasted how soft her mouth was. His demands tempered slightly as the supple curves of her body molded into his.

The sweetness of her soft mouth fought with his anger and won. His groan became a low moan as his body filled with need. Desire gentled his ravaging, but even as both his lips and his touch softened, his demands increased. Any thought of stopping vanished the moment he felt her lean in, when he could feel the want in her response.

The way her hips moved against him, searching, seeking that perfect fit. His growl deepened. Allowing both hands to languorously caress her perfect form, he worshiped her curves boldly.

Her whimper eased, permitting soft moans to chorus with his, until his thumb swept over a peaked nipple as his hand filled heavily with her velvety breast. Lia gasped, the sudden sharp intake sucking cool air around the heat of his lips.

Heaven. Oh God, Heaven

He couldn't believe he was thinking that one word. But he was.

Damn.

And then, Damn.

Mute felt the prick against his ribs a second after Lia's body tensed, her roaming hands deserting him. Abruptly he stilled. She backed from his arms even as they dropped to his side.

Lia was breathing heavily, grabbing massive gasps of air, the sound of it filling the space around them. She faced him, his own knife once more in her possession, waving it at him, her body semi-crouched and ready. Her eyes were wary, but as he studied her, an unaccustomed elation assailed him with far more damage than any she could physically inflict upon him.

"Don't!" Her voice dripped with ice.

"Don't what?" There was a hint of humor in his deep voice, but his face didn't show it.

"Don't do that." Lia's chest heaved, drinking in much-needed oxygen. "Don't touch me."

Although not an easy feat, Mute allowed the left side of his mouth to gently curl. Still, his voice was strong. "Not unless you want me to." His gaze traveled over her face, pausing on trembling, swollen lips before landing on her soul-filled eyes, eyes filled with apprehension, fatigue, anger.

And desire.

The fire in his blood surged.

It was written all over her face. Not even her scowl could hide the heat lingering in those amber depths. Lia didn't want to want him. But want him, she did.

He didn't say anything. Didn't move. Didn't even shrug. Mute only stepped back a step to distract her before lunging, clasping her wrist tight within his grip and stripping her of his knife before she got the bright idea to try and kill him.

Again.

Side-stepping around and then behind her, he let go of her wrist. Wrapping one arm around her abdomen, he pulled her back fully into his chest, ignoring the pain in his ribs created by the abrupt movement. He bent his head slightly and slowly, purposely, nibbled at her delicious throat. He let his lips travel only a moment before he stopped, drinking deep, breathing her sweet fragrance in. The pain in his ribs paled into almost non-existence as he relished this one, single perk of this job. Deliberately he hesitated a full second, savoring how her body sighed into his before he whispered into her ear. "You'll have to beg me." Certainty rang in his husky voice. He knew, without a doubt, one day this woman would. His arms relaxed.

Relief replaced the wariness on her face when he allowed her to nimbly exit his embrace. She rubbed at the wrist he had commandeered. She spat out an adamant, "Good. Then it'll never happen. I don't need to worry about that on top of everything else."

Mute started to chuckle but didn't. It would only trouble her.

Besides, it wasn't in his nature.

Eight

Four hours, twenty-two minutes, and six seconds later Mute had a decision to make. The outskirts of Baki loomed before them. Contact would be made here. Nevertheless, the decision facing him now weighed heavily upon his broad shoulders. He had the choice of contacting DuPries directly, requesting transport, or he could ask a friend for a favor.

The favor would cost him dearly.

In his business, a favor could mean anything. Anything at all. At any time.

Even death.

One asked only if there was no other option. The question remained---whether the alternative, DuPries, would exact a higher price.

Mute positioned Lia under a grove of Hornbeam trees squatting under a lonely rim far from Baki. He gave her a long look while calculating risks and determining the best of his limited choices, certain nothing, as usual, showed on his face.

Lia unexpectedly pursed her lips as her eyes bombarded him with sudden animosity. She went ballistic, her words spewing out. "Don't even think about it." An abrupt movement of her arms lifted her bound hands as if they could somehow attack him from their imprisonment, from behind her back. Something he'd felt more comfortable with since her last attack.

Mute hesitated, without understanding why.

Lia's eyes cut into his, those amber globes darkening to burnished gold as they filled with hatred, and a touch of sorrow. Her shoulders squared as did that stubborn perfect chin. Mute tried not to stare as even that sexy little mole above her sensuous lips tormented him.

"Don't you dare." Her face suddenly contorted, fatigue again reigning as she pleaded. "For God's sake. Don't. Whatever you're planning. Don't."

Mute remained immobile, although had the emotion he was feeling been apparent, he would have shaken his head in puzzlement. He had no idea why she was adamantly against his plans for he had not voiced them.

Or why she was scared.

But she was. Enough for her breath to shorten. Enough that her body trembled.

"You think you…" Lia never got the chance to finish her request.

Again, Mute had no choice.

None.

Giving her temple a slight tap with a closed fist, he knocked her out cold.

He could only stare as consciousness faded from her, her eyes slipping high and back into her head as her body slumped. Her body relaxing as she fell against the back of the tree she was tethered to.

For the first time in his life, he wished for a different line of work. A full-on grimace replaced his normally unreadable expression. Silently cursing, he checked her bonds, making sure his captive was secure, with no possibility of escape.

Silently he warred with himself and then stopped. What was the point? After all, he knew full well the job before him and what it took to accomplish it.

Speaking to his contact was mandatory and he couldn't march a handcuffed, bound prisoner into that world.

Questions would surface. Questions he didn't want. Or need.

Mute let his gaze consume the now unconscious prisoner before he abruptly shifted, turning toward his destination. Even as his body traveled, fully intent on the mission, his mind remained with the slumped, unconscious form of one Lia Von Stratham.

Nine

Lia awoke slowly.

Oh. My. God. How her body hurt. Her muscles protested wildly as she struggled to consciousness. She gave up the attempt to stretch and shrugged off the pain.

Not an easy task. But she did it.

Lia's pulse sped as she remembered where she was and how she'd gotten here. Not to mention, why she'd again lost some time.

The last few days swamped her memories. Hopelessness threatened to overwhelm her as she recounted her dilemma. The capture. The forced travel. The indignity of losing her freedom. The uncertainty of the immediate future, or even, any future at all.

Glancing around her, Lia gathered information. She was still a prisoner, tied to a short, stubby tree. Night flickered a waning greeting as it crept past. Millions upon millions of twinkling stars bathed her in their light, blinking brightly in the broadest, blackest sky she had ever seen. A scene worthy of a Time magazine cover, but one she couldn't enjoy for her world held only darkness.

And hopelessness.

Lia gazed at the distant lights of the city as though it were her last night upon this earth. And it most certainly could be. A sudden fervent cry sprung to her lips. But she curbed it quickly.

Lia needed strength. She needed control. She needed to detach herself from the emotion she was feeling. This helplessness. The hopelessness.

Anger started. And Lia allowed the feeling to magnify, to grow and blossom.

She forgot everything but the fact she was tied to a tree in the middle of fricking nowhere, in the middle of fricking nowhere Asia, in the middle of God forsaken fricking nowhere Asia, in the middle of God forsaken no fricking where....

Her chest heaved. Her heart pounded. Her eyes bore every ounce, every trace of raw detestation when her captor emerged from the black night. Lia chose to remain silent as his powerful, purposeful body crept closer.

For the moment.

Only when she gouged him with molten eyes did her voice surface. "You hit me."

When he didn't acknowledge her statement, Lia's eyes brimmed, with actual tears. Not for her, but for him. How could anyone be that unfeeling? That cold?

Their eyes locked.

Something flickered in his. And then he blinked, and that nanosecond of humanity was gone.

"Sorry." His voice was so soft Lia almost didn't hear his apology. She certainly wasn't convinced of his sincerity. His answer wasn't expected or wanted. But it silenced her as nothing else could have.

She accepted his callous shove as he pulled her to her feet. She forced tired legs to move when he tugged her along an invisible path toward the lights.

Lia no longer cared where they were going. Her best hope was that maybe, just maybe, this nightmare would be over soon. She glanced at his impassive face, noting the tiredness etched in unrelenting lines. Although few, if any, would understand the lines written there in his expression, she did.

After days in this man's company, she had learned to read one or two of his incomprehensible expressions. Now was no exception.

This man had no desire to continue. Mute no longer wanted anything to do with this assignment. Whatever he had found out from his little trip had changed his mind about this mission. It was obvious he had decided the payoff was no longer worth the trouble of dragging her to wherever his employer had designated.

He no longer wanted anything to do with it. He no longer wanted anything to do with her.

Anything, at all.

With her.

Ten

Mute loaded his prisoner into the back seat of his newly acquired 1969 Moretti 128 Roadster; his clenched jaw the only visible indication he was a tad bit unhappy with this particular collection of nuts and bolts. At least it had four bald tires and an engine that ran.

Occasionally.

Years of abuse had only enhanced its original butt-ugliness. But the fact remained---his choices had been limited to this one particular butt-ugliness.

Tethering Lia's hands to what didn't even pass for a passenger seat, an actual crate turned upside down, he decided the exterior of this rust bucket was a significant improvement over the interior. The back seat was a handmade burlap job that had long ago lost most of its stuffing through a multitude of rips and tears.

"Ah, first class." A soft snort accompanied the derision-filled comment coming from his captive.

Mute only pushed her further into the rear seat before he slid behind the wheel. He ignored the metal springs poking into his back and prayed the car would start. They needed to be miles from here by morning.

"Where are we going?" Lia's voice rose above the grinding clunks as the motor coughed and hacked its way to life.

Mute pressed down on the gas pedal slightly, letting the engine warm for a full minute before he shifted it into gear.

"I asked---where are we going?" Lia's tone dripped with sarcasm.

Mute glanced back at her, specifically, at her long, stiff, feminine back. He didn't particularly like that she had to face the rear because of her restraints, but it was her own fault.

He couldn't take the chance she would try to kill him. Again. Not while he was driving.

At least she was lying down.

He ordered, "Get some sleep."

"Thank you. I will." The woman had no intention of obeying his command, and it was evident in her sticky, saccharine tone. Mute didn't have to see her to know she had opened her mouth to ask again, but he was surprised she only took a long, deep breath. He enjoyed a full minute of silence.

"Where are we going?" Her voice had gentled. Hearing the mix of curiosity and resolve made a part of him soften and he hated that. Or maybe he was unaccustomed to it. Regardless, it was there. And it took a lot of effort to get rid of it.

Steeling his mindset, he asked necessary questions. "What do you know about Rulin International?" For once, intensity replaced his usual lethargic tone.

Surprise caught in Lia's throat, making her stumble over her words. "Ruin what?" When he didn't repeat his question, she asked again, correcting her pronunciation. "Rulin International What?"

"What do you know about Rulin International or its CEO, Stepan Kovolev?" Mute asked.

"Stephen who?"

"Stepan Kovolev." He enunciated carefully.

Lia, sounding dazed, repeated. "Stepan Kovolev?" Her hesitation was obvious. "No, I don't know anyone by that name." She paused for a moment. "Why?"

"You've heard me speak of him before. Marcel DuPries is the name he used when he hired me."

Her words sounded as drained as his body felt. "I've told you a thousand times. I don't know any DuPries." Her words slowed to a cautious crawl. "I have no idea why anyone would pay you to kidnap me." Her tone flattened, indicating she had said the words far too many times before. "No idea. None."

Silence grew as Mute pondered the details. It wasn't that his employer had left out necessary facts. The man hadn't. It wasn't that his employer had lied about his identity. Nothing unusual about that. But red flags were popping up everywhere. What would a multi-billionaire who ran one of the world's largest munitions company want with Suzy Nobody?

He'd learned her entire life's history when she'd chosen to infuriate him by talking nonstop for an entire day. She had rattled off every glorious detail of a very ordinary and perfect suburban American upbringing just east of Trenton, New Jersey, with two wonderful parents and a zoo of pets and strays. How her sheltered and nurturing childhood had been the reason she had wanted to help those less fortunate. How she had ended up working for Global Outreach.

Helping those who'd never had the opportunity for hope.

"Who is Stepan Kovolev?" Her voice wafted gently to his ears as if she wasn't entirely speaking to him.

"He owns Rulin International." Mute's right foot eased, allowing the car to safely navigate a left turn. Nonetheless, he wound up eating a fair amount of road through the open window as the car slowed, allowing the dust to swirl and settle on every surface, including his open mouth. He spit before continuing. "They manufacture weapons, munitions, body armor, and tactical gear. Major clients include a dozen military factions as well as police and security from across the world, as well as surveillance companies." He could go on and on, but Lia didn't need to know more.

"What is the plant's location?" Lia asked.

"The company holds operations in several countries. Germany, France, Egypt, Russia." That list grew as well.

"What would the owner of a weapons factory want with me?" Her voice cracked.

This woman was as innocent as one could be. Suddenly, Mute knew Lia Von Stratham was just that---innocent.

Still, the question remained. One requiring answers. "Yes. Exactly. What would the CEO of one of the largest companies in the world want with you?"

"Do you seriously think I stole a file from the head honcho of a mega-conglomerate?" Indignation tinged her tone.

Mute knew she hadn't. But admitting it wasn't in the game plan. "Doesn't matter. I don't get paid to think."

"If I paid you, what would your answer be?"

For a split second, he wanted to laugh.

And anything resembling mirth was such a bizarre feeling that Mute physically started. He glanced around, toward Lia's back. Amazingly, the woman had somehow maneuvered into what had to be an extremely uncomfortable position. One that allowed her to stare back at him. He caught the honesty in her eyes. Lia really wanted to know if he thought her a thief. His heart beat picked up. For a long moment, he was the one captured. Somehow, managing to elude her stare, he shook his head, again focusing on the road.

He didn't answer. He couldn't. Normally he chose to remain silent, but right now he couldn't have uttered one single word had his life depended on it. Mute couldn't remember the last time his opinion about a mission mattered, or if ever.

He heard her sink back into a reclining position, his ears picking up the release of a bedraggled sigh.

"I didn't steal anything." Lia's tone softened, but the conviction behind the words was far more convincing than had she shouted.

Mute let the silence grow. But he heard every breath and every sigh from his prisoner. He knew the minute she fell into a fitful, but much needed, sleep.

He turned his attention to the road ahead, and not just the one he and this car from hell were bouncing down. The one Marcel DuPries had started him down.

The one ending with Stepan Kovolev.

Eleven

Sunlight ripped through Lia's suddenly transparent eyelids. She squinted against its onslaught before burying her head into the mattress, desperately wanting to block out the light. *Five more minutes. Just five more minutes.*

Turning her head away from the light, her cheek instantly flamed, burning from the roughness of the burlap scraping it. Her eyes sprang open. It took a moment to remember she wasn't in her warm, cozy bed back home. A soft groan surfaced as she reached to check the damage to her face, when, oh crap, her restraints tightened against her still healing wrists.

Yeow.

The groan became a growl. Captivity was infuriating. Finding her wrists still tied behind her, Lia's growl morphed into a roar.

It bit at her soul to be unable to move, much less to check the damage. Lia took a deep breath, hoping to calm her racing heart. The memories before sleep claimed her kicked in and she raised her head, trying to determine where they were.

Apparently, they had stopped. An ancient high-winged Cessna was parked nearby, its dingy ecru exterior broken by leftover bits of faded blue and red stripes. There was the distinct biting scent of aviation fuel in the air, supporting the fact they were at some sort of airport. She knew this even before she

observed hangers constructed about the same year
Khufu built the great Pyramid.

Mute was nowhere in sight.

Or so she thought.

Abruptly he was in her face, tugging her arm
with one hand even as the other deftly freed her from
her restraints. He pulled her out with the efficiency of
a wet seal gliding through crisp, cool water, while she
exited with as much grace as an ox lumbering through
its first ballet lesson. Mute's hard face held no
greeting as he untied her hands. She unconsciously
acknowledged that distinct *or else* in his terse
command.

"Try anything and I'll knock you out and drag
you." He'd already proven the truth behind this
particular declaration. Twice.

Lia showered him with a withering glare
before finding herself herded toward an awaiting
plane. Her heart beat started to pound. *Finally, a
chance to escape. This is it. Surely there's someone
here who can help me. There just has to be.*

Lia focused on remaining calm and compliant,
steeling her face into impassiveness, beating down
her heartbeat so she wouldn't miss any opportunity to
escape. And she had every intention of pulling from
the iron grip holding her arm and taking her chances
with the pilot.

Until she got a look at the burly, surly shell of
what used to be a man.

Bloodshot eyes ogled her, and she had to fight
the urge to wrinkle her nose at the noxious vapors of
sweat, gin, and, oh yuck, was that urine? Vomit? Lia
barely concealed a grimace as she strove to find

oxygen. A grimy, oil-stained baseball cap was perched jauntily atop a greasy, tangled mess of salt and pepper fiber no longer resembling hair.

But when this man leered at her, his wide hit and miss of a toothy grin shining at her, Lia physically shuddered, feeling violated by his gawking stare. Her stomach heaved as the pilot's roving gaze lingered in all the wrong places.

She involuntarily succumbed to the desire to protectively fold her arms over her chest.

"Howdy, ma'am. I'm Murray." The man held out a grubby hand toward her. Lia clamped down real aversion. She was grateful when Mute abruptly stepped between her and the pilot. Although previously inconceivable, she threw Mute an *I'm indebted to you forever* glance.

Not that it mattered, for her captor wasn't looking at her. Mute appeared totally focused on the pilot.

Murray continued his introduction as if her reaction were completely normal. "It's a real pleasure to be in the company of such feminine beauty." The man licked his lips, the gleam in his eyes sickly bright.

Mute's mouth hardened, but Lia was having difficulty focusing attention on her abductor. She was trying desperately to squelch the uprising in her suddenly queasy stomach and barely heard Mute's tense order as he commanded, "Just get us to Qena."

The man's sneering grin never faltered. His gaze remained on Lia, bypassing her face, instead traveling over her entire body. "You bet." His eyes became mere slits and his sneer deepened sadistically.

Lia's pulse started to climb, even more so at his next words. Words aimed at her companion even though those lecherous eyes never left her body. "I'll do it for free if you give me half an hour with her."

"No." Mute's harsh voice negated the possibility even before he stepped completely in front of Lia, blocking her from view.

The man looked up at Mute as if seeing him for the first time, squinty eyes blinking hard before narrowing. Something resembling realization passed over his gray face. "Tapping that well yourself, are ya?" His archaic, wiry body postured, fists fully clenched. For an instant, Lia was afraid Murray was going to strike Mute.

However, after sputtering a loud, explosive curse, the man deflated. Spinning abruptly, he led them to the aircraft. Mute had to drag her forward for her knees were shaking too hard to walk.

For the first time in days, Lia was absolutely thrilled to be in Mute's company. She humbly followed his every step, letting him lift her into the plane and fasten her seat belt, absolutely delighted when he took the seat next to hers.

Once the plane had climbed into the spasmodic cottony clouds lazing in a clear, azure sky, Mute had closed his eyes. Lia knew he was asleep. Or rather what she had come to consider Mute's sleep-mode. In the past few days, she'd learned this man didn't sleep the way a normal person could, or would. Although he allowed his body to rest, neither his brain nor his senses ever did.

Mute sleep-mode meant he was as aware in sleep as most were when awake. She didn't understand how the man was capable of such control, but she had seen it time and time again.

Taking advantage of the current situation, Lia allowed one small desire. She let her eyes roam all over this man. Every hard angle, every rough edge. Covering every square inch of him, from that dark hazel wavy hair, that planed, etched face, his mottled t-shirt covered muscles, before sliding down to those strong as tree trunks camo covered legs. Lia lifted her head and again focused on his chiseled, handsome face. He'd shaved yesterday using that huge knife, so technically the stubble was only a day old, but still it looked like two. Dark. And as hard as he was. Creeping up the sharp angles of those sculpted cheeks.

Subconsciously she found herself studying his mouth. That narrow, intense upper lip a sharp contrast to his full, sensual bottom one. Right now, both were flattened from the wariness only she could sense in his half lounging repose. But the passion she'd felt from them augmented her heightened senses, and Lia had to fight the heat filling her. Tamping down the molten memories that sensual mouth had created took a mountain of effort.

And right now, Lia wasn't up to the task. Her breathing shortened and then deepened. Her heart began to hammer in her chest. Looking away before a fire in her flamed, she found she couldn't. Her gaze seemed magnetically drawn to him as she again studied the man who singlehandedly kidnapped her, and would deliver her to what could only be, at the very least, dire circumstances, and at worst, her death.

There was an aristocratic air in that long, patrician nose, but it had been broken one too many times for anyone to ever consider it true or straight. Nevertheless, imperfect fit his strong face. It toned down that model gorgeousness to a more manageable, just downright handsome level in that virile, masculine way of his. She let her gaze travel over him, taking in every detail of his dark, chiseled face, his honed, ready body.

Lia knew first hand of the brutality of this man. She'd suffered at his mercy far more than she wanted. But a small fraction of her understood him, recognized his objective, his motivation, and the willingness to carry out the mission. He was fulfilling the duties of a job he had agreed to do. No more, no less.

And that element of her was the part that followed the contours of his face, the planes of his cheekbones, the lines etching that sultry mouth, lines visibly shouting to the world of his essence and character.

Sleaze unexpectedly filled her ears, pulling her from the wonders and complexity of her immediate perusal. She stiffened, bracing as the pilot's words assaulted her.

"You know, sweetheart, I can make you soar in ways you haven't even dreamed about." The slimy words had the effect of ice water being flung over Lia's entire body. She shivered for a moment before facing the scum-bucket flying the plane. There wasn't any way in hell she was going to let this man's words get the best of her.

Lia turned, finding Murray's attention on her, not on the vast sky before them. He flipped a switch, and she read the controls. Auto pilot. Uneasiness began to seep into her pores.

Murray leered at her, his eyes consuming her, roaming from her breasts to the apex of her thighs. Lia fought the urge to cover herself with her hands.

"He doesn't have to know, dearie." The man flicked a glance at Mute, the reclining giant sleeping beside her, before visually attacking her with another lascivious stare.

Lia fought the bile rising in her throat even as Murray swiveled in his seat and reached for her. She suddenly found herself fending off a grimy hand as it grabbed at her breast. She didn't have time to think, only react.

Her eyes narrowed on her adversary even as her right hand slid Mute's knife from the sheath hanging on his belt. Lia's mouth tightened as she jerked the weapon to the pilot's open throat, the blade's tip sinking in just deep enough a single drop of blood peeped. And then grew from that grimy, gritty leathery skin. Her voice sounded more of a hiss than actual words. "Autopilot off. You fly the plane."

Lia felt Mute stir beside her, even though it wasn't a physical movement. But she didn't look at him, her attention centered on Murray, waiting for the leech to comply. Her body felt as tight as newly strung wire.

Mute's deep voice, along with his disdain at being disturbed, sluggishly penetrated her concentration. "Sweetheart." He stressed the word, although his tone was strictly conversational. "Mind the jugular." A soft sigh feigned exasperation. "It's been a few years since I've flown anything this small."

Suddenly, inexplicably, Lia wanted to sink the blade deep within the degenerate masquerading as humanity who'd harassed her. That tiny drop of blood blossomed, becoming a steady stream as the tip of her knife bit deeper into flesh.

Automatically appalled by the vertical necklace of ruby red blood, Lia felt herself back off, allowing the flow of blood to slow. Still, her piercing gaze remained centered on the vile piece of garbage that had accosted her. And she kept the blade at his neck.

Murray's red rimmed eyes widened, full of terror. Not only from the knife, but from the conviction behind her action. Her hand remained in place, the cold edge of steel against a vulnerable throat.

Murray's wide eyes screamed his fear. They pleaded, begging for life, such as it was.

It was enough to catch Lia's attention.

With effort, she found her voice, and it rasped with injustice. Ignoring her insecurities, Lia answered Mute, her tone hard, purposeful. "Now, darling, you know perfectly well you can fly anything with wings." Her tone dripped syrup. "Even this piece of crap."

Mute shifted in his seat, gracefully maneuvering from repose to upright. Deftly, and without hesitation, he swiped the knife from Lia's grip, his eyes conveying the full meaning of *Don't kill the Pilot* as he fit the knife into its sheath. A habit he apparently found humorous for, although he didn't smile, there was just the barest hint of laughter in his dark gaze.

Lia felt her shoulders slump as Mute pulled her arm down to hang by her side, once again resuming control. As if none of this nightmare had happened.

His face resumed its usual bored vigil.

Lia's breathing quickened. Her eyes narrowed. Not on her attacker, but on the man beside her.

How dare he treat this attack on her... this assault... this threat of rape as inconsequential. Without warning, the urge to slap his handsome mug got the best of her.

She swung.

Hard. Connecting solidly to his honed cheek. Hard enough to ring, even above the roar of the engine.

Mute's black eyes darkened, the depth in them startling. Although he remained immobile, his stiff body shouted retribution even as his cheek flamed, a bright red, raw, ugly hand print appearing on its stubbled surface.

It took two full seconds before Lia realized what she had done. And then her own eyes widened, becoming saucers, while the frown crossing Mute's lips had flattened to less than a line.

A thread of steel deepened his tone although his voice remained deceptively calm. "Sweetheart, let the man fly the plane." Both brows furrowed above his nose. "At least until we get to Qena."

Lia's pulse raced. What had she done? Clarity of her actions and reactions hit her at once. She'd drawn blood. Used a weapon. Threatened a life. And not only that. She'd physically harmed another human being. By her own hand.

Lia looked down at her stinging palm before her eyes crept to the red hand print etched on Mute's unbreakable jaw.

A chill settled in her heart, causing her body to tremble. Her head hung. She had never thought herself capable of harming another human being. Ever.

Lia's mind instinctively argued key points, needing solid reason for her actions. Defense had been the primary cause of the violence. And with good reason. A slow boil fired the blood in her veins, banishing the shivers. Never had she had to defend herself before. It wasn't her fault she'd been thrust in that perverted man's path. She didn't choose to be here. Would never have chosen this. The need for justice overwhelmed her. Lia's hackles grew.

She had no reason to be sorry. Turning to the man who'd become her jailor, she could feel her face burn scarlet with rage.

This was his fault.

Still, Murray was no longer a threat. The future concerned her more than the past. Her voice lowered, although still quietly yelling volumes, "And what awaits us in Qena?"

"Another car." Mute's typical indolent tone was back. Meaning he was done answering questions. He affirmed it by ordering, "Get some sleep."

Lia deflated as Mute threw a warning glare at the now reticent pilot, for it meant he was once more in complete control. Leaning back heavily, her eyes closed as she fought to swallow the wrath filling her. It didn't go down easily, hitting her stomach full force. She drank in a giant breath, striving for composure. Eventually, she felt calm enough to open her eyes and start again with her questions. Answers were her only salvation.

Turning, Lia once again focused on the now resting Mute. His eyes were closed, mouth vaguely slack, those strong shoulders relaxed, arms folded over his massive chest. Her eyes grazed his red cheek, the shape of her hand vividly outlined on his face.

Anger immediately vanished, remorse replacing it with just as much fervor. Without realizing it, her fingers reached to sooth the damaged skin.

She couldn't help herself. Her words were barely audible, and sounded far too raw and husky. "I'm sorry. I shouldn't have hit you." Lia stiffly waited for a reaction.

Mute opened one eye a mere crack as he passively studied her. Without emotion of any sort, that one eyelid returned to its original position, closed.

His unfathomable expression never wavered.

Lia dropped her hand.

And then her head. It was no good trying to talk to him. She didn't know why she bothered. Sighing deep, she settled in for the duration and after giving Murray another threatening glance, she decided to take advantage of the situation and try to rest. It might be a long time before another opportunity presented itself. Her mind reviewed the endless miles they had already covered in the previous days, and her body relaxed even further. Yeah, sleep sounded like a grand idea.

Forcing the tension away, her breathing slowed as the exhaustion, both mental and physical, took over. She was just about in dream land when she thought she heard Mute's low deep voice.

"You get one more." There was an infinitesimal touch of mirth in his tone.

Lia had to rouse herself, but she did so quickly. "What did you say?" As customary, he didn't answer. His eyes remained shut, and his position never changed. Nothing about the man suggested he'd even heard her request. Still, she hoped for a reply. She asked again, "One more what?"

"One more and we're even." The man exhibited absolutely no movement other than his lips, his body completely relaxed into Mute sleep-mode. Whatever humor had been present before, was gone. Completely.

Lia let out a long, "Ah, I see." Tentatively, she lay a hand on his broad shoulder, finding it suddenly tense under her fingers, although the shifting of muscles was completely invisible. She understood the significance of Mute's words, remembering full well he'd knocked her cold and unconscious twice already.

"I don't do revenge," Lia stated bluntly, her body stiffening. "It costs too much." A small sigh escaped, the breath easing away slowly as her body loosened. Regret over her lack of restraint lowered her voice into a barely perceptible whisper. "I really am sorry."

Mute's full lower lip thinned until it was a mere scratch. Black as night eyes flew open even as his hand shot out and grabbed her wrist, instantly flinging her hand from his shoulder. "Don't."

How this man managed to yell while whispering was beyond her. Lia's eyes rounded wide as she struggled to comprehend. "Don't what?"

Mute visibly calmed, returning to his usual languid state.

And Lia wondered how he could be a tyrant one second and completely controlled the next. But her surprise skyrocketed when he answered her query.

"Don't apologize." His dark gaze finally settled, locking onto hers, all that usual remoteness gone. A surreal hardness etched in it until Lia reeled from the intensity.

She'd honestly thought he didn't want her to touch him. Baffled the reason went deeper, she asked, "Why not?"

No answer.

She struggled with her apology, for reasons having nothing to do with making her voice work. "I'm sorry, Mute. I really am." Her hand hovered just above his arm. "I had no right to…"

"I said… don't apologize." His clenched jaw strangled the words but the meaning was crystal clear for those, in this singularly rare moment, intense black eyes threatened her with certain doom. His body shifted away from her.

Lia's eyebrows puckered. "But I'm sorry. Really sor…"

"I said. Don't." His low, hard voice held steel--cold, brittle, unbreakable steel.

A slow shaking of her head began as comprehension seeped into her brain. Lia's face, as well as her heart, softened.

Apologies were only necessary for people who actually felt something. Anything. Forgiveness doesn't matter if you don't care. What had happened to this man to have sucked all life from him?

Lia's eyes burned suddenly as her hand slowly lowered to rest beside her thigh. Watching him relax, sinking into the hard seat and closing his eyes, further instilled the depth of this man's isolation from the world. And from her.

Lia forced herself to do the same, although her mind raced with questions. And *not* a whole hell of a lot of them dealing with their next destination. It took time and effort, but Lia finally fell into an uneasy sleep.

Apparently, all her hard work paid off for an insistent voice rang in her ears what only seemed minutes later, even though several hours had passed. "Wake up sleeping beauty." Someone's hot hand was briskly shaking her shoulder. Lia forced one eye open. Then the other. Just in time to see Mute glowering at her as he began to pull her from the seat.

Lia wasn't given a chance to stretch away the cramps created by her recent confinement, for she was immediately whisked to an awaiting vehicle. At least this one had been produced in this century. She prayed for real seats.

Luck decided to shine and lo and behold, it did.

Even better, Mute let her sit in the front. Albeit, with both hands handcuffed to a bar installed in the dash, apparently for such purpose. But it was significantly better than their last conveyance, where she'd been strapped to a burlap seat, backward. Grateful, and more importantly, because Murray was nowhere in sight, she flashed Mute a blinding smile. Lia wouldn't have to deal with that scum bag again. Definitely reason enough to smile.

The smile faded when Mute backed away from the car, a dark scowl on his face. Abruptly he locked the doors and then headed to the nearest hanger, leaving her to sweat in this her latest prison.

Twelve

It had taken twenty-seven minutes to scrounge up a phone, make several calls to known contacts, inquiring about Kovolev. The last call, to Kovolev himself, had taken less than one.

Mute unlocked the car door, and slid behind the wheel without glancing at his passenger. He didn't like the instructions he'd been ordered to follow. They were to fly, after a road trip to Sohag, into Sibiu, and from there a chartered plane would be waiting, on standby, to fly the pair to Moscow, where DuPries, or rather Kovolev, would be waiting. It left much to the mercy of his employer. An option Mute was no longer willing to accept.

Even with Lia's impossible, but numerous and mindboggling scenarios of reasons someone wanted her, it still didn't make sense why Kovolev needed a relief worker to the point of kidnapping one. None whatsoever.

And the lack of information from his usual contacts appeared entirely genuine. The motivation behind this job was a well-kept secret. Kovolev was keeping this close to the vest, whatever this was. Mute's only option was to play into Kovolev's hand.

For a little while longer.

Mute sucked in a breath. This shit was new territory for him. What the hell was he thinking? Trying to figure out what an employer wanted with the package. What difference did it make? He was in this for the money and nothing else.

This was so not his style. He did his job and that was that. He clamped in a suddenly threatening growl.

Of course, Lia chose that precise moment to gaze up at him, those amber eyes bright with expectation and wonder. Her sensuous lips remained closed, but the question was written all over her face. *What now? What else am I to endure?* Even that dark, sexy dot perched above her upper lip seemed to question his motives.

Mute steeled himself against the pull of her. He hardened every fiber in his being against the query in her soul-seeking eyes. His body tensed as he strove for the control necessary to carry out this mission.

But mission parameters had changed. He'd never reneged on a deal before, but the subjects of previous missions were always scumbags the world was better off without. The only question now was how to protect his package from DuPries slash Kovolev.

Mute followed gut instincts and mentally calculated alternative options. Deciding which avenues would be best, he pulled out his phone and got to work. By the time they landed in Sohag, contingency plans were in place. And ready.

Mute felt better. Plans B and C and, if necessary, D gave him options. Enough that he felt able to surrender to Kovolev's transportation selection.

Within hours, they were in final descent into the tiny airport in Sibiu. A chartered plane was waiting for them. They were to board and fly to Moscow. Something Mute fully intended.

Kind of.

The minute the plane touched ground, Mute jerked Lia up and toward the exit. Clasping tightly to her upper arm, he waited impatiently until the door was finally opened. Roughly dragging her out, he ignored her muffled protests at the indignity of being manhandled.

The second his feet hit concrete, he called to Kovolev's escort, who'd been waiting to lead them to the next conveyance. "Gotta find the ladies room." He gave the hulking bouncer type a conspiratorial wink, pulling Lia beside him to the point she was almost running. They were inside the main terminal before the man could protest.

Mute whispered to Lia, "We're going to the bathroom. I need to make a phone call. Make it look good."

Lia gawked at him, her mouth dropping open. But she shut it quickly and nodded. It was gratifying to see the determination settling in her suddenly straight back as well as a hefty measure of resolve lifting a stubborn chin. Although she wanted to ask questions, several of them if he was reading the cogwheels in her brain correctly, her lips remained sealed.

Grateful the lady was cooperating, Mute pulled her into the women's restroom and ignored the startled women now racing to exit. Shoving Lia into a stall, he pulled out his phone, checking his messages. Thankfully, the one he needed had come through.

Mute skimmed the terse instructions. Checking the fourth stall on the left he found the requested items in a small duffle behind the toilet. If he had been the type, a huge sigh of relief would have escaped him. But he wasn't, and he only opened the duffle, confirming the requested items were inside.

They were.

He zipped up the duffle with determination, the distinctive sound loud in the silent bathroom. Then a toilet flushed. It was then he sighed. Lia had taken advantage of the situation. Good for her.

Mute heard the door open. Quickly, he shoved the duffle out of sight, before finding bouncer man lounging against the entrance door, an expectant gleam in inquiring eyes. Composing his voice lethargic took little effort. "Make sure she doesn't try to escape while I do the same." He waited until bouncer man rested his eyes on the emerging Lia before again stepping into the stall. Without shutting the door, his back in plain sight, he relieved himself, the noise covering the transference of the contents of the duffle into the compartments and pockets of his pants. When finished, he exited the stall and found both Lia and bouncer man waiting. He only nodded, making for the door, leaving the now empty duffle behind. His voice was curt. "I'm ready. Let's go."

He was ready.

For what was coming.

They were almost to the end of the last hall when the attack began. Three hulking, angrily determined men leaped toward them, springing from a side door, their intent faces hidden behind long beards traditionally grown by locals. Insolent eyes promised extreme consequences if Mute and Lia were taken.

However, Mute had no intention of allowing that particular scenario. He pulled a semi-automatic from behind his back and let loose, getting two in two quick bursts of fire. Bouncer guy had a pit bull grip on Lia's arm with no intention of letting go. Mute put a bullet behind the closest ear. Blood and tissue sprayed onto Lia's face, and she jerked automatically. Mute didn't have time to sympathize. He still had one more assailant to deal with.

He chose to make it personal for he'd hated the leering gleam in the man's eyes when the man had first glimpsed Lia. This piece of trash would have used her every which way and then Sunday before delivering, or killing her. This scum didn't deserve to do so much as breath.

Dropping the automatic weapon, he reached for the huge knife Lia always seemed to prefer.

The blade glinted wickedly at the man, who still held his gun, up and ready. Mute never hesitated, thrusting his entire body at the man, his blade sinking deftly into the jugular even as gunfire rang from the weapon. For a moment, Mute went completely still as an unaccustomed thought consumed him---even stray bullets could hit Lia. Never before had unintentional targets mattered to him.

A giant, strangled snarl surged up from previously unknown depths as Mute abruptly snapped the neck of the man he was holding. Grateful the gun was slipping from lifeless hands, now silent and non-threatening.

He spun, searching desperately for Lia.

Although Lia's eyes held every bit of the shock she felt, it was also just as obvious, the woman was very pleased with the outcome.

It hit to his core that those amber eyes held relief and an immense gratification for his saving her. Relieved to still be his prisoner.

And thankful.

He fought for sanity as the urge to hug her close, assuring himself she was no longer in danger, surfaced. Although the adrenaline in his system screamed the opposite, Mute kept his arms from reaching for Lia.

He refused to give into the stupidity seeking to destroy his common sense or his way of life. It didn't matter which. But he had to admit, it was welcoming to find Lia grateful to be his prisoner instead of afraid or angry.

An unaccustomed tenderness swamped him. He made sure it wasn't in his eyes before focusing on her blood-splattered face. Reaching, he touched her cheek, drawing his fingers lightly over the hollows, swiping away the gore.

Lia blinked, her body tightening to the point of breaking. Her sharp intake of breath dominated the silence. "Don't."

Mute stilled, his hand inches from her face.

Lia's features stiffened. "I… I will clean…" Her voice cracked, her eyes suddenly brimming. "I'll clean up the blood you spilled."

Mute's body spiked back as if it had taken a stomach punch. And again, strange emotions filled him, as well as the desire to defend his chosen profession along with the practices necessary to be successful in this vocation. But one look at Lia's stoic, innocent face kept his mouth shut. He unconsciously let out a soft sigh, perceptive enough to know few were accustomed to the rules he lived by.

Mute ignored her request. Her quivering chin shouted it was only bravado stiffening her back. Easily grasping this was a feeble attempt to return to normality, he understood her rejection wasn't of him, but to the brutality of his life.

A large part of him softened. He spat into his fingers and allowed his touch to wipe some of the grime and blood from her face, never letting her eyes stray from his. Something deliberate must have shown from them for Lia's breath caught and held. His hand reached again for her cheek.

She jerked back, away from his touch.

His glare seared into hers, locking their stare. A very real and suddenly vehement part of him demanded her acceptance, enough so, he grabbed Lia, holding on for dear life. His grip remained unbreakable, fingers forceful and uncompromising. His eyes drilled her with superhuman force as he silently requested her to accept his world.

A world full of danger. A world of corruption. A world of death.

Long moments passed as he continued to clean her face, each stroke gentler than the last until they became caresses, and she had time to adjust from her sinless world into his dark and often bloody one.

Lia's amber eyes darkened. And then swam with unshed tears. But they didn't falter. Her resolute gaze remained locked on his as her unspoken acceptance finally filled those soulful eyes.

His heart flipped in his chest as her acceptance flooded him. Mute's soul soared for the first time in his life. He smiled down at her. Or rather, even though his lips remained frozenly flat, he thought he had.

But the most unexpected effect happened.

His nonexistent smile materialized in his eyes. For the first time ever, those black, lackluster eyes twinkled. Revealing everything he was feeling and more.

Enough so both Lia and Mute lost their breath.

And both understood the significance.

Mute went dumbfounded and silent.

And then his heart stopped for a moment, as Lia's lips lifted into a hesitant smile.

Still, he could read the question in her eyes.

The one asking what did it matter if he, her kidnapper, the man apparently leading her to a lengthy and horrible demise, cared one iota about her existence?

Yet he did. He knew he did.

And had just proved it.

Hadn't he?

Thirteen

Standing in the fresh, powdery snow covering Moscow, Mute cradled the phone in one steady hand as a cryptic voice asked about progress. Mute's own tone was just as harsh. "I'm bringing her in." His hesitation was deliberate. "My way."

There was an unwelcome stillness over the static. Finally, a rough, accented voice acknowledged. "Your fee is waiting."

Mute gave a satisfied grunt, although his mouth hardened. Other men would have made another declaration as proof of dominance, but Mute didn't feel the need.

He made for the safe house via a series of routes to ensure they were not being followed, although the house was one a reliable connection had made available. Munitions and supplies, as well as appropriate clothing, were waiting.

Ten minutes later he chained Lia to a towel rack in the bathroom while he searched the place. With an experienced eye and a handy little electronic device, he searched for bugs of the most inconvenient sort. When he found nothing, Mute double-checked again. Only then did he ascertain the items he'd requested were indeed at the ready. Doing a double check was automatic, but he went through the items again, to make absolutely sure it was all there.

But he was only stalling the inevitable.

Finally, he stood in front of his prisoner.

Lia looked up at him, eyes begging, wanting the impossible from him. And for what seemed the millionth time, he hardened his heart against the pull of those beautiful, innocent, always questioning gold eyes, eyes pleading with him to forgo his mission and release her.

A small measure of comfort rose within him as, once again, she accepted the denial in his eyes. Like Hell, he would let her go. His mission had changed, but he still had to deliver her to Kovolev. If he didn't, Kovolev would just send someone else to recapture Lia. No, he had to find out why Kovolev wanted her. It was the only way to protect her. Besides, he wasn't ready to release his captive. There was more to Lia. More to be learned. More to…

Mute squelched his racing mind. The more he knew Lia Von Stratham, the more he wanted. And that knowledge taunted as nothing ever had before.

Being deceived about the mission left no lasting impression, for it had happened far too many times to count. It was part and parcel of the job.

This betrayal begged questions, though. Questions only his employer had the answers to. Answers that would only be revealed by completing the mission of handing Lia over to Kovolev.

Even though the mission was the same, the outcome had changed. And the part that should have bothered him was the money, extravagant money, he'd lose.

But for Lia Von Stratham.

Not a problem.

He searched his prisoner's eloquent face and understood Lia didn't know what was worse---

remaining trussed up and hauled around like garbage, or the fact she would soon be standing before the Russian who had instigated her kidnapping.

Without a word, he withdrew a key from his pocket and unlocked the handcuffs, again admiring this woman as she stood. She didn't rub her wrists or verbally attack him. Nor did she appear vindictive about being bound. Turning his back to her, he led the way into the sparse, utilitarian living room before gesturing for her to sit on the sofa. Lia refused, remaining in the center of the room. He waited for her to check out escape possibilities, but her puzzled gaze remained on him.

Mute was ready for the question.

"Why does he want me?"

He accepted the desperation behind her words. But more importantly, he recognized her real question. The one asking what was he going to do with her next?

Mute allowed his God-given talent to silently shout-the-obvious relay his message of full sanctuary.

Lia obviously understood and, without question, accepted. Mute could only guess at the resolve behind Lia's apparently ready belief.

Unexpectedly, she lifted her hands in front of her, waiting for him to tether them again. The gesture wasn't acquisition, but one of trust.

A part of him humbled.

Mute was shocked by the emotion flooding Lia. Her face was an open book. Confidence and trust were supplanted with determination. He knew the exact moment her strength of resolve lessened.

Although she was by far the strongest person he had ever encountered, even Lia felt trepidation.

The unknown was just that, unknown. He could see the sliver of fear sparking in her eyes.

Without thinking of the consequences, Mute did something he never thought he'd do. His strong, able arms wrapped themselves around her soft shoulders before he whispered huskily, "I won't let them hurt you."

Lia, although nodding, pulled back and out of his embrace. Her eyes glazed as if holding back tears, but they remained fastened on his, questioning. Her tremulous voice finally emerged, "You know, however much I want to believe that..." A gut-deep sigh exploded from her sensuous lips. "I can't."

A strong emotion walloped him, one he couldn't name. Regardless of how much he had shielded himself in the past, today he couldn't help himself. Feelings, hot and fully alive filled his mind and his blood.

Something stilled the desire to struggle against the flood. Mute was suddenly aware he no longer wanted to let life, nor the pleasure of feeling, ebb on past.

Enveloping her within his arms, he pressed his lips against her temple. She felt like heaven, all warm and soft. He breathed deep, filling his lungs with her delicate, sweet scent. He knew full well the impression he was giving, but even with all his training and experience, dammit, he couldn't help it. Mute suddenly wanted to join the living. He wanted some of that zeal and gusto-for-life that centered Lia.

And he wanted more.

He wanted her. But more than that, he wanted her to want him. He wanted her to accept him, all of him.

He wanted her to love him.

The realization made his body stiffen.

Lia's face jerked up, and puzzled eyes bore into his. He made sure his wore its usual blank mask.

"You're going to give me to Kovolev?"

Long moments passed before he answered. "Yes. I have to."

Lia snorted indelicately, pulling out of his embrace. "You have to?"

"If I don't, someone else will."

"What do you mean? Someone else?"

Mute looked at the floor. His feet shifted and then re-shifted. The tone of his voice dropped, somehow both shaky and firm. "Kovolev wants you. He will send as many as it takes to get his hands on you."

Lia's mouth rounded. "But why?"

Mute raked a hand through his hair. "That's what we don't know. And why I have to take you to him." Inwardly, he flinched at her involuntary shudder. "Only when we know the why, will we be able to figure out how to stop him." Locking her gaze with an intense one of his own, he vowed, "Permanently."

Mute stepped toward the couch and dug through the bag of equipment that had been left for him. "I have no intention of leaving you there, but until we change his mind, he will never leave you alone."

"How are we going to *change his mind*?" Doubt tinged her every word.

He wanted to tell her everything was going to be okay, that he had a plan, in fact several plans, but he kept his lips closed and only shrugged. It startled him, enough so that, when Lia's soft touch gripped his upper arm, she was able to jerk his body around until they were facing each other.

"I'll ask again. How are we going to change Kovolev's mind?" Determination hardened her tone and her attitude.

Mute shrugged again, stalling. Finally, he spoke. "That depends on the reason for his interest in you."

She let out an exasperated sigh, threw her hands up and then quickly down, before planting clenched fists onto her hips. "Okay, you can stop with the one-liners." She lifted her hand, one long, slender index finger pointing at him. "I want to know how you intend on getting me out of there... wherever there is... alive. And I want to know now." She huffed, her bountiful chest heaving. "And I have no intention of dragging it out of you, one word at a time. Got that, Geronimo?"

Mute suddenly grinned. It was slight, but it was real. He saluted the diminutive beauty. "Yes, sir." Clearing his throat, he began. "I've got a plan."

Lia waited, but Mute didn't elaborate. Impatience got the better of her and she stomped over to him. Clenched teeth made her words gravelly. "I thought I made myself perfectly clear. Tell me the plan."

Mute shook his head. "No. You can't tell what you don't know."

It took several long moments. Moments where puzzlement and then comprehension played with her face, before she deflated, wrapping slender arms tightly around her torso. "You think I'll be tortured?"

He stiffened. "Not if I can help it."

Lia continued to stare at him for several moments and he returned to task, shoving a full clip into the Glock in his hand. Mute checked his watch. "We leave in twenty."

Lia's whisper was breathless and ragged. "Where are we going?"

"To the address Kovolev sent me."

Abruptly Lia paled and then bent over, clamping both hands on her knees. "Excuse me…" She made a bee-line for the bathroom, one hand clutching her stomach.

Mute followed at a more sedate pace. He frowned at the sound of Lia's retching. He was the cause of her nausea and he hated it. Finding a washcloth, he held it under cool water, wrung out the excess, and then placed it on the back of Lia's neck. Gently taking over the task of holding her hair out of the way, he declared, "It's going to be okay."

Was that really his voice sounding so tender and soft? But it continued, even lower and gentler than before. "I promise everything is going to be all right." For some previously unknown reason, he repeated his promise, the action searing his soul. "Everything will be all right. I promise."

Fourteen

Fingers tightened into fists as Stepan Kovolev ended the call. Amber eyes flamed hotly before he could rein in his temper. He glared at the black rectangle in his hand for a long moment before pinning his uncle, Helmut Schmidt, with a furious glare. Despite the havoc threatening to consume the majority of his gray cells, his voice remained calm. "All is not lost, Onkle." Cruel lips thinned into a solitary line before a quick breath returned them to their normal smile-infused position. "Our man is bringing her in."

He stuffed the phone into the pockets of an Armani dove gray suit, complete with a paisley pink silk tie before his voice smoothed silkily. "It seems our man has no desire to lose the last half of his promised fee."

"Ah, Goot." Helmut Schmidt's hawkish features relaxed. The elderly scientist dug into the right pocket of his lab coat, producing an old-fashioned cotton handkerchief and then wiped a wrinkled brow. Still, as if knowing success was in the details, Schmidt prodded, "An when is dat?"

"Soon, Onkle." Stepan's eyes began a slow twinkling before brightening into tarnished gold. "Very soon, indeed." The younger man speared his uncle with a triumphant glare.

A shadow appeared across Stepan's face as Lucienne Dubois unfolded her tall, lithe frame from a snow-white Eames Lounger. Dressed in black silk from head to toe, she elegantly slithered around the massive clear acrylic desk to stand beside Stepan.

Her ballerina-like grace captivated Stepan for an instant and, as always, he marveled at the classic beauty. The combination of a dancer's elegance with a merciless killer's instinct never failed to excite both his blood and his libido. He rarely cared in which order. His gaze settled on luscious, full lips as she spoke with a soft, accented voice that almost purred.

Her fingers trailed up his jacket lapel in a familiar, seductive manner. "Ah. The wait is almost over." An evil glint sparked in pale green, almond shaped eyes. Eyes already highlighted by straight dark-as-night hair pulled back at the nape of her long, slender neck. "Finalement." Her pronunciation of the word slipped off her tongue like music even as the malicious gleam in her eyes sharpened.

Stepan's heartbeat picked up as desire filled his blood. Not for the pleasures of Lucienne's body, but from the promise he recognized in those unholy green eyes. But before he could respond, Onkle interrupted.

Schmidt barked a sharp report, mimicking laughter, although the sound was far too brittle to succeed. "Goot. Goot." Bespectacled eyes narrowed, squinting to mere slivers. "Your sister has proven a challenge, has she not?"

Stepan didn't answer, aware the elderly scientist hadn't included Lucienne in his question. Schmidt held no love for Lucienne and, from the disgust on his assistant's face, she him. Dismissing this trivial matter from his mind, he began working out another strategic maneuver or two to counter this latest development.

"Yah? Stepan?" His uncle, not receiving an answer, prompted loudly and forcefully, a hard gaze threatening to slice the younger man into halves.

Shaken out of his revelry, Stepan turned to his uncle. A sardonic smile turned full lips up even as his eyes hardened, seeming to freeze in place. Their glacial gaze emphasizing the planes of his angelic face. "Yes, Onkle, she has." A wicked smile grew. "But she will no longer." Stepan had taken great pains to ensure his twin would be arriving soon. He beamed, knowing his dream, his plans, in fact, all he lived for, were now within reach.

Stepan's amber eyes glowed with satisfaction at the actuality of his dream coming to life. His entire body pulsed with pleasure, even as the gleam in his eyes hardened.

Lia Von Stratham was almost his.

Fifteen

The streets were congested, making their progress slow, giving Lia far too much time to think. Her frown deepened. She, better than most, knew how proficient Mute could be, but a nagging slip of a thought seeped to the front of her worries, refusing to go away.

There wasn't any disk. So, the real motive behind this Kovolev person wanting her was anyone's guess. Why someone would want her so badly as to kidnap her was beyond sane reasoning. It was impossible to know the why without all the pieces of the puzzle.

But anyone willing to go to such lengths wasn't the sort who cared how she would feel about it.

No. This man, whoever Kovolev was, had only sinister intentions for her. A shiver ran down her spine, and she trembled violently for a moment.

Mute must have felt her shudder for he softly asked, "You okay?" His arm snaked around her shoulders, one hand rubbing up and down her upper arm, hard and swift, but gentle and tender at the same time. She relaxed into him, soaking up all his protective warmth, as well as a healthy dose of masculine brawn and virility.

And the significance of her automatic response hit her square in the heart.

As Lia's eyes roamed over his honed face, her fears subsided. The man was incredible---skilled, proficient, and deadly. If anyone could save her, it was Mute. She swallowed hard, and found comfort in his ability and strength, before nodding.

Mute's strong arm cocooned her, his breath hot against her skin as he whispered, "It will be over soon."

Lia swallowed as if she was trying to get something unblocked from her throat. Again, she nodded.

The words were choked. And abrupt, for she had the hardest time getting them past her lips. "I know." Her eyes pleaded with his. "I'm just…" Her gaze dropped to her feet. "Scared."

Mute chuckled.

Really, he did.

And then he stiffened.

It was obvious Mute found his verbal outburst far more unbelievable than she ever would. And his face proved her discovery for his eyes were suddenly wide and utterly readable. Still, the man was able to determine her evident hesitancy for what it was.

Dark eyes lasered into hers, as if the man proclaimed the most profound truth. "Never have I met anyone braver, Lia Von Stratham." His typical grimace returned. "But you have every reason to be afraid."

Something in his gaze communicated a real reluctance to continue their mission, the one handing her over to Kovolev. "Things can go very wrong, Lia." His voice tightened. "If they do… Fight. Fight hard." He laid a tender touch on her cheek. "Stay alive, Lia." Piercing eyes reinforced the directive. "I don't care what it takes." That low voice deepened to whisper soft. "Just stay… Alive."

Lia couldn't look away from those mesmerizing dark orbs. She cradled her hand within his, holding it against her face. Words refused to come. But her mouth opened, widened, and fought for the words. Suddenly, she knew exactly how a fish out of water felt, and how ineffectual gasping out of your element was. Her mouth was moving. But words wouldn't come.

"I will get you out of this." Mute's voice was low, hesitant, but completely confident. "I promise."

Sixteen

Stepan Kovolev studied the giant towering over him with offhanded impudence. But it was the woman standing slightly behind the hired-help, who sparked the gleam in his malevolent eyes. A sneer threatened as he correctly perceived the unabashed astonishment from the pair before him.

Lia's beautiful face was incredulous, while the mercenary he had hired, swiveled a curious gaze back and forth between Stepan and his twin, the study as deliberate as its intensity.

Stepan decided a brotherly approach would be fun. He took a step closer and opened wide arms. "Ah, dear sister. How wonderful for you to come for a visit."

Lia's hands locked in front of her torso as if she were trying to stop their shaking. She stammered. "B... B... Brother?"

A sardonic grin lifted one side of Stepan's lips. "Yes, my dear."

He liked how Lia had paled at his greeting even as the giant hovering beside her seemed only vaguely interested. The man's eyes had widened slightly before returning to their blank, ambiguous normality.

Lia took a half step back, now absently wringing her hands, as frightened eyes centered on him. "I don't have a brother," she began.

Stepan interrupted. "Surely you don't deny the resemblance?" Her face was identical to his, the same structure, the same mouth, the same eyes. Eyes he had never seen before, but nevertheless, were the same ones which stared back at him in the mirror every day. Striking a pose, he preened, his hands smoothing his stylish coiffure before tugging the opposite sleeve cuff, straightening his immaculately pressed sleeves. "I have to admit. You are *even* better looking than I expected."

A rush of desire filled him. And, for a moment, Stepan wondered at the possibility of making love to one's self. His gaze traveled over his sister in a slow, languishing fashion. He so loved his own image.

The mercenary, standing beside his sister, tensed slightly.

Stepan's regard swung to Mute's impassive form. Few would have been able to read the signals, but this man held some kind of emotional tie to his sister. Instinctively, Stepan knew it as fact.

No matter. He'd lifted his leg on a couple of females in his time. Rolling one shoulder, he concluded this matter could be resolved at a later date. For now, there were other pressing issues. Stepan placed a leather case on the desk and pushed it toward the pair.

Stepan turned to Mute. "I believe you want this." It was a statement.

Mute crossed the room and flipped the briefcase's latches, opening it wide enough to determine the contents. He threw Stepan a casual glance. "Pleasure doing business with you."

One of the two chairs in front of the crystal desk swiveled. Lucienne rose with cat-like nimbleness, crossing to inspect Mute. "Yummy." Slender fingers played across Mute's broad chest. Her generous mouth was turned into a wide smile, but it held no warmth. The brittleness in her eyes matched the malice in Stepan's.

A soft purr resonated slowly up her throat and finally from behind full lips. "Won't you introduce us, Stepan? I've waited a very long time to meet your dear, dear sister." Her eyes remained locked with Mute's for another second or two before her gaze homed in on Stepan's sister. Lucienne moved toward Lia with a grace generally reserved for those schooled, from birth, for the ballet. One hand traipsed elegantly up Lia's right arm, long fingers skimming lightly.

Lia gasped and shrank even further.

Stepan's voice was belligerent. "Lucienne, my sister, Lia." He waved a weak hand at the woman in black. "This is Lucienne Dubois. My..." His slight hesitation was interrupted.

"Everything." Lucienne finished for him, a wide, wicked smile swinging between both Lia and Stepan. Her fingers were still trekking along Lia as they traveled across her shoulders, her back, and then down her other arm, the woman creeping around Lia's still form. There was an unwholesome glaze in her eyes when she finally met Lia's terrified ones.

Lia yanked her arm from Lucienne's touch and shot across the room, toward Mute, shouting at Stepan. "Why would my brother pay to have me brought before him?" Those amber eyes, so much like his own, held a wealth of defiance alongside the obvious fear. "Why not just introduce yourself and ask?" Probably because he didn't respond, she demanded an answer. "Why, brother? Why?"

Stepan no longer felt the need to hide the truth now that she was his to control. "I take it you wouldn't believe it to be brotherly love?" He chuckled, the sound harsh and evil. "No, I don't expect you would."

Lia blew.

An explosion of bottled resentment mingled with hatred spewed from set lips, as Lia crossed her arms over her chest. "There's not a chance in hell." The endearment turned into a sneer. "Brother."

"Ah, sister. We're going to have such a good time getting to know one another." The gleam in Stepan's eyes promised. But he was fully aware the man he'd hired to capture her had stiffened into paralysis even though the mercenary ebbed complete and total indifference to the conversation.

Stepan hadn't gotten where he was by ignoring instincts. And he intuitively knew this man was going to be a problem.

But he thoroughly enjoyed toying with his victims as much as felines did.

His lips lifted. "Ah, my lovely sister." His steely voice grated tenderly on the word sister. "What other reason would I have for bringing you here if not brotherly love?"

Lia didn't answer.

Mute spoke, interrupting the silence, his voice hard. "Lia doesn't have a brother."

Stepan jerked toward the speaker. And a slow smile got the better of him, surprised at, not only the servant's perception but the man's unlikely question. "No?"

Without hesitation, Stepan spun, dropping his pants to show everyone in the room his left butt cheek, revealing a crisp, hard-edged tattoo, the exact mirror image of Lia's.

Lia gasped loudly.

Mute only tensed. And then Lia crumpled, almost falling into Mute. He barely had time to catch her.

Stepan laughed, but there was no mirth in it. "So, you're beginning to believe me?" Turning his head to read their puzzled faces, it was gratifying to discover both were sufficiently stunned. He pulled up his pants, fastened them and then strode around the large desk.

Letting his rear rest against the edge, he cleared his throat and began. "Our father genetically engineered us." He pointed at her and then at himself. "We were created for a purpose, my dear sister. You and I." He watched his sister carefully. "We were created."

Lia turned a pea shade of green. Mute held her up even as a dangerous look crossed those hard features. The mercenary remained still. Intent. And ready.

Stepan refused to stop, loving the pain he was inflicting. A pain he had always had to endure. "That's right, my beloved sister." He ground out the words. "We were created. Not conceived." A sharp, hollow laugh filled the room before Stepan continued.

"Our father was a brilliant man. Absolutely brilliant. A visionary, to say the least. A man with the ability to bring about peace. World peace." Another leer slipped off thin lips as Stepan's eyes narrowed. "Although his notions were honorable..." A sly grin got the better of him. "They weren't exactly profitable."

Stepan stood suddenly, as Lucienne gracefully moved to join him, leaning into him, one slender hand resting lightly on his upper arm. "Father gave me the paradigm, but you will supply the means to the end."

Lia froze. "I don't understand."

Again, Stepan chuckled, a blatant sneer contorting his face. He loved when Lia's terror developed into full horror. "I'm sure you don't," he agreed amicably. "However, it remains that, with your help, I'll be able to..." The glint in his eyes hardened. "Rule the world."

Seventeen

Mute had dealt with delusional before, but never this level of insanity.

A quiver of fear began creeping up his nerves. It was all he could do to keep his hands off Lia. He only wanted to wrap his arms around her and protect her the only way he knew how. With his body. But that wasn't going to happen. They had to play the game a little longer. And play it smarter. Meaning his employer couldn't know how far he was willing to go to protect her.

Although it went against every grain, Mute took a half step away from Lia. He had to keep Kovolev from suspecting his plan. It was going to be hard even if he caught Kovolev completely off guard. If the man had an inkling---Mute couldn't think about failure. Not now.

There had been two guards at the main entrance. Not a problem. There had been two more in a side room filled with monitors. Not a problem. Two more were stationed on the other side of the door to this office. Not a problem.

The problem was the two in this room, for they had their guns trained on him. It was impossible to surprise anyone in full view. Amazingly, when he'd been searched upon entry, they had discovered every weapon. When Kovolev had hired him, the man had stated he only hired the best. Apparently, Kovolev occasionally told the truth.

Mute's mind worked a few scenarios, discarding all until he settled on the best option for escape. All the while listening to Stepan's chilling voice as the bastard baited Lia.

Stepan continued, "I, too, had no idea I had a twin, for I was raised without siblings. I was adopted from birth, as you were. It was only when I could not activate the final sequence in Pet that started me down the path of enlightenment." Stepan's shoulders rocked slightly as he gave an eerie sound, supposedly a chuckle. He explained, "Pet is my nickname for my…" He corrected, sweeping a hand to indicate an elderly man who had just hobbled into the room, coming to stand far too close to Lia. The white lab coat brushed against Lia's leg as the man's beady eyes scanned her face as if she were a germ under a magnifying glass.

Stepan corrected, the emphasis conveying resigned reluctance to share. "*Our* greatest achievement." And then he purposely marched to Lia, throwing one arm around her tense shoulders, pulling her toward the man she had instinctively backed away from. His leering grin deepened as his head dipped toward hers, his eyes gleaming wickedly. "Let me introduce you to Onkle." His arm tightened. "Lia, this is Helmut Schmidt. Our father's former assistant and our unofficial uncle. It was Herr Schmidt who arranged for our adoptions." Allowing Lia to scramble from his embrace, he turned to Onkle. "Herr Schmidt introduced me to father's invention. It was he who determined it is only by combining our DNA that I can unlock the key that has evaded me for so long."

Lia opened her mouth to speak, but Stepan interrupted, adding, "Father knew his invention had the potential to be what some call a..." his pause defined effectual. "World annihilation weapon."

Lia's face went ashen as Stepan continued. "Yes, you heard right. It is capable of extinction on a planetary scale." Moving to stand behind his desk, Stepan reached for a black, rectangular device. "Here, let me show you."

Pressing a sequence of buttons caused part of the far wall to retract into the ceiling. The view went on forever, showcasing a large warehouse-sized laboratory, complete with dozens of white-coated people moving about computers and equipment placed at the edges of the building. All were tiny compared to the center structure, a giant ball-like device resting on a massive steel cylinder. Three smaller poles emerged from the top of the sphere, completing a rough triangular point.

"Would you like to see it in operation?" Stepan's voice was breathy and his face brightened with an unholy anticipation.

The sphere started to vibrate while the poles began to shift, aligning.

In the lab, people looked up, first at the ball, and then in their direction. A mad scramble began as the scientists dove for computer stations. A giant screen transformed the wall at the end of the building and on it, a countdown instigated. The digital numbers were a good four feet tall. They began at Five minutes and included not only minutes and seconds, but Deci seconds, the numbers spinning almost faster than comprehensible.

Lia stood motionless and ashen, her gaze locked on the sphere.

Mute kept his expression lazy even as his heart began to pound in his chest. There was a devilish glint in Stepan's eyes, one proving the man had no intention of stopping.

"At the moment, it's trained on one of the thousands of obsolete satellites orbiting the earth, but the destruction is hard to see, so…" Stepan pushed several buttons, and the sphere began to rotate. "How about I change the target to, oh, I don't know, something small, like Uganda, or maybe, Sri Lanka."

Lia suddenly turned, clamping him with a pleading glare. "No! Don't!" She took an automatic step toward Stepan. "Please, I believe you. Don't. Please."

Stepan's smile widened.

The countdown hit twenty seconds.

Lia surprised Stepan when she rushed over, gripped his arm tightly and then yanked it down. "No. Stop. You've got to stop it. Now!"

The countdown read five seconds. Four. Three. Two.

Mute could feel his body stiffening, his hands balling into fists. It took everything in him to remain still.

Stepan searched Lia's terrified face, locked onto her transfixed stare for another second.

And then keyed one button.

The huge digital clock froze.

The sphere ceased vibrating, and the poles relaxed into their initial position.

The giant numbers on the opposite wall stood at less than half a second.

Stepan laughed, the sound maniacal and grating.

Mute's shoulders drooped and he let his head hang before anyone could see the desperation he could feel swallowing him.

The man was a psychotic lunatic. A maniacal psychopath. Totally unhinged. Stepan Kovolev was beyond deranged.

He, and Lia, were screwed.

Eighteen

Mute's heart slowly returned to normal as he studied Lia's insane brother. The man was certifiable, and he knew, with absolute certainty, you can't reason with crazy people. So, talking wasn't optional as a means of escape. Flight seemed to be the best choice.

And now, while everyone was distracted by Stepan's little show, seemed to be as good as any.

The two goons blocked both doors so that only left the window overlooking the laboratory. It was huge, taking up most of the wall and the dimension was in his favor. It was doubtful Stepan had installed a bullet-proof grade window inside his own building, especially one this ginormous. Now, if he could just get Lia's attention, and coax her away from Stepan, and closer to him.

"Impressive." Mute kept his voice conversational. When Lia turned to him, incredulity stamped on her lovely features, he gave her the tiniest of nods and jerked his gaze down to the floor left of his feet. Quick as lightning, he looked back up at the identical twins.

Damn. He was fairly certain Lia hadn't understood his signal.

But her brother had.

Stepan sneered as he took Lia's elbow in his hand and began to lead her toward the massive window, right where Mute wanted her. Stepan was taunting him, and he knew it.

Mute sidestepped, closing the distance to the pair.

"Ah, yes. Isn't it?" Stepan's cruel smile matched the foreboding gleam in his amber eyes. "But the best is yet to come. Isn't it, dear sister?"

Lia appeared to find some backbone. "And what is that?"

"Exactly what I said." Stepan casually gestured to the giant orb. "When you can annihilate entire cities, you can control the world." Again, that haunting chuckle made Mute's blood turn cold. "Even more so when you can destroy the entire planet."

Mute let his head cock to one side. "Won't killing yourself in the process defeat your ultimate goal?"

Helmut Schmidt, who had previously kept to the shadows, reminded every one of his presence. "Ah, that's the beauty of Heinrich's genius." The little man removed his spectacles and absently began to clean the lens with a cotton handkerchief he'd removed from his lab coat pocket. "Heinrich, their father…" He pointed to both Lia and Stepan, "Perfected a way to infuse blood using TSA, a transitory epidermal application, one capable of penetrating all five stratum levels. Using pre-programed qualifiers, we can interrupt the way human cells read DNA." Schmidt lifted the glasses up, studied them in the light, and then gave a little grunt of satisfaction before again settling them on the bridge of his nose. Taking a deep breath, he continued. "During translation, an mRNA sequence is read using the genetic code. The genetic code is a set of three-letter combinations of nucleotides called codons. The start codon in all mRNA molecules has the sequence AUG and…"

Stepan interrupted with a short, irritated growl. "Enough." He strode to his desk and again picked up the remote. "Suffice it to say, we are able to 'infect' the human population. All mankind will die. With the exception of a handful of carefully selected individuals I personally have chosen."

"Then your little presentation was just that---a show?" Mute kept his voice bland.

Stepan turned to address Lia. "Did you not want to see why you were delivered? Did you not want to know why you are so important? Central enough to have you brought to me?"

Mute didn't like the grin Stepan was giving his sister. There was far too much malice in it.

Lia's eyes narrowed, and her shoulders tensed. "You haven't explained how I fit in this… this… abominable picture." Defiantly, she folded her arms over her chest. "Is it my blood? Or is it my DNA?"

Stepan's eyes cut to Onkle and then refocused on Lia. "You have nothing to fear, dear sister." He thumbed in Mute's direction. "He was given specific orders to bring you in unharmed. And, as I, um, we…" He nodded at Schmidt. "Will have to DE-sequence your DNA and run several tests, time is in your favor." An evil grin slowly grew into a lecherous smile. "Which will give us plenty of time to become well acquainted." His smile hardened. "Very well acquainted. So well, in fact, your usefulness may lengthen your stay with us." Abruptly, he moved to lean against the acrylic desk.

Stepan punched a button on the remote, and the soft whir of a motor filled the strained silence. The window covering began to lower.

Mute knew it was now or never. Leaping toward the desk, he reached for Lia, pulling her by his side, before picking up one of the swivel chairs and hurling it at the glass.

Both guards sprang into action. The one with the nasty scar across his nose leaped for Stepan, tugging the man behind his large frame. Helmut Schmidt shrieked and ran for the closest door, the back of his hand warding off another scream. Stepan's face turned hard and maniacal, even as he accepted his bodyguard's silent order to remain behind his human shield.

Mute had been prepared for a loud crash as the glass broke, but only a dull thud was heard. Stunned, he glanced at the unbroken window. Had there been time, he would have allowed his jaw to drop. Apparently, Stepan took absolutely no chances whatsoever. Mute's eyes narrowed. He couldn't remember the last time he had underestimated an opponent.

Or if ever.

Plan B would have to be initialized. And that meant a door. Grabbing Lia's hand, he bolted for Helmut Schmidt and the far door. The other guard, who reminded Mute of a Pit Bull, leaped around the desk to his right, so he went left, leaving Schmidt's door the logical choice. Lia must have figured out the same plan for, thankfully, she matched him step for step. Pitbull jumped onto the desk, taking a short cut, and the paraphernalia on top went flying, scattering in every direction, crashing noisily.

Stepan screamed. "Catch her. Catch her. She is Vital!"

Lucienne threw Mute a maniacal smile as she lazily stepped toward him.

Mute pushed Lia toward the door, yelling, "Run."

Lia put on a burst of speed at the same time a hand caught at Mute's forearm. He turned and landed a solid right on Pit Bull, who was trying to catch him in a bear hug. Out of the corner of his eye, he caught Lia flying past Schmidt as she threw open the door. Schmidt held his handkerchief in front of his face, only his wild bespectacled eyes showing. Mute thought about smiling at the fright in them.

But he didn't have time. Pit Bull was doing his best to spin him. Giving Lia time, Mute obliged and clocked the guard again with another right. The man staggered back, unable to get a blow in.

Mute took advantage of the reprieve and headed for the same door Lia had used.

Suddenly, pinpricks hit the center of his back. His mind whirled, but the predominant thought was for Lia. He silently screamed, *Run,* even as what felt like thousands of volts electrified his body. Looking over his shoulder, he caught the malicious enjoyment in Lucienne's smile as she held one finger on the Taser controller before he fell, face-planting and seized. Before the seizure was over, the volts hit again.

And then again. And again.

Drool ran from his mouth. Snot pooled under his nose and lips. His tongue hung to one side. His eyes were half-closed, one far more than the other, and he couldn't focus. When his body finally stilled, he could hear his own panting. It sounded as if he had just finished an all-day run. Finally able to move, he rolled over onto his back. When he could see something other than white sparks, Mute's stomach knotted.

Stepan's and Lucienne's taunting faces hovered high above him, each holding a smirk, promising unbearable torture and pain. Mute closed his eyes.

"What a shame." Lucienne made a tsk, tsk sound.

Mute fought against the laughter rising within him. Of course, he'd never had a problem keeping silent. Still, his face loosened, almost relaxing.

Something Stepan must have found irritating for the man's face reddened, and his eyes narrowed. His voice sounded as if he were talking around a throat filled with river rock. "You should have taken the money. You could have been a rich man. An alive rich man." He sneered. "Now, you'll find my generosity extends just as much, but in a very different direction." He nodded to Pitbull. "Take him to the cellar. I'll want to talk to him in a little while." His smile turned repugnant. "Please have him ready for our little, ah, discussion."

The guard nodded.

Mute stiffened as he was none too gently lifted off the floor. Scar grinned without any mirth, joining Pit Bull, both grabbing his inner upper arms.

They dragged him to the door and exited, but not before Mute got a glimpse of a bedraggled Lia being pulled into the room. She was being held by the outer guards. One held both of her hands behind her, forcing her to move in front of him as the other steered her in the right direction. Toward trouble. Toward Stepan.

Mute lunged for her. Or thought he did. But his legs, still tingling, refused to budge. All he could do was drown in those scared, sad, questioning amber eyes, eyes holding his. And for the first time in his life, he knew his were as scared as hers. He mouthed the words to her. Silent words.

Stay alive.

Just stay alive.

Lia's eyes filled, the torrent streaming down suddenly gaunt cheeks.

Mute groaned, the sound loud enough to drown Stepan's greeting to his sister. And then his groan mutated into a growl. Fastening onto Stepan's widening eyes, he hurled an ultimatum. "You hurt her and your death will be slow." He was being dragged from the room, but his eyes remained locked on Stepan's cruel ones.

Stepan laughed, the sound brittle, calculated, and entirely evil. "My sister and I are going to have so much fun."

Somewhere, from depths previously untapped, Mute found the strength to lunge at Stepan. For the first time in his life, his face transformed with feeling, his eyes burning with rage, and an insane fever, to save Lia. The force of it was potent enough to get his limbs to respond. Mute sprang for her and almost broke free of his captors.

Almost.

Lucienne pounced, one black booted foot sweeping up so fast he didn't see it. His face felt it when she kicked him so hard his jaw shifted. He stumbled. And then one of Lia's guards hurried to assist, throwing his body heavily into Mute's, and with the help of the other two, had Mute, once more, manhandled into submission. His cry was strangled. "Lia… stay… alive." The last words were thrown toward her as he was dragged out and then down a narrow hall.

Out of sight of either Lia or Stepan, Mute wasn't sure who benefited the most from being denied the sight of torture. He suspected Lia, for Stepan was most likely the sort to order suffering and pain.

Pitbull tossed Mute a mocking grin before removing a pair of brass knuckles from a pant pocket. The grin grew as the other two held Mute outstretched between them, both locking his arms in a position against the wall. The guard took a giant breath before delivering his first punch.

The thud of a blow upon soft flesh sounded loud in the small space. Pitbull's grin widened even further. Mute's eyes watered. Somehow, he kept the groan inside, even as more blows landed.

Enduring each punishing blow, Mute forced his mind to shut out the pain.

It centered on Lia. What was Stepan doing to her now? Would she be able to endure her diabolical brother? Did she have the fortitude to survive?

And more importantly, how was he going to get her out of this?

After what seemed hours of punch after horrendous punch, in truth, long, long minutes, Mute was tossed into an eight by eight-foot holding cell. He fell heavily on the hard stone floor. Lying still for several moments, he was able to catch small, tiny breaths. He didn't need a doctor to know his sprained ribs were no longer sprained and wondered exactly how many were broken. Still, he was grateful neither lung had been punctured. Tentatively, for it hurt to raise his hand, he felt his puffing face. His nose was broken. Again. Which didn't worry him as much as the lost teeth he had already spit out. Squinting through swollen slits, he surveyed his new home.

The only item in the room was an old, rusty bucket. No windows. No bars, only stone walls. Graffiti covered the entire wall space, even the ceiling, indicating previous occupants.

Not a good sign.

The only way out was the door. Turning his full attention to the solid structure, he studied it. It was metal, and thick, by the looks of it. There was a four by eighteen-inch slot in the lower fifth of the door, assumedly for food and water, if prisoners were given any. He frowned slightly as the realization hit him. There wasn't a key hole, or handle, on this side. None. The plate was entirely smooth.

Shit.

That left only one very undesirable escape route.

Through a guard. His only chance for escape would be when someone opened the door. He openly cursed for this tactic couldn't be mapped. There wouldn't be any strategy other than hope-for-the-best. There was no way to know how many guards were stationed where, or which route was an actual exit.

The question remained.

How could he break out, find and rescue Lia, along with saving the world from Stepan's insane plans?

And Stepan Kovolev needed to be eliminated if Lia didn't have to run for the rest of her life. Kovolev would never quit trying for Lia. Never.

Which only left---Kovolev must die. As much as Mute hated the thought of killing Lia's only biological family, only Stepan's death would ensure her safety.

Every cell in Mute's already taut body tightened.

Cringing against the pain, he waited.

His opportunity would come.

He only hoped it would be soon enough.

To save Lia.

Nineteen

Lia's heart strummed loudly in her ears. It was as if nothing in this world could quiet it. She barely heard the order to remove Mute from their presence. When it finally registered, her body sank. Only the stiff, unyielding arms of the guards kept her from slipping to the floor.

Stepan's sardonic voice filled the air. "Now, dear sister, we can get acquainted, you and I."

Lia glared at him, her spine straightening, as his real meaning hit her. She spat out the words. "One introduction was quite enough." Clenched teeth grated the final word. "Brother."

Stepan's laugh was demonic. He nodded, and the goon holding her dropped his hands. The suddenness startled her, and she almost fell. But something inside her tightened and she managed to remain upright.

And that strength enabled her to scowl at her brother. "Don't think for one minute I will go along with your plan." Her glare intensified. "I don't care what it takes. You will never have my cooperation."

Stepan's evil smile widened.

The sight infuriated Lia. So much so, she decided to educate her brother. "Even if it means my…" her voice hardened, dropping to almost a whisper, "Death." She swallowed, for her mouth was suddenly dry as chalk. "I will kill myself before I let you continue."

Stepan laughed, the sound harsh and diabolical. "Don't worry, dear Sister. I won't allow any harm to befall you, regardless of whose hands." His eyes sharpened

His glance shifted to another guard, the one who resembled Disney's Tasmanian Devil, for the man was wide at the shoulders and had short legs which made his arms seem to hang to the floor. Stepan jerked both his chin and his eyes to the door.

Taz nodded.

Lia found herself escorted out of Stepan's office and down a short hall. She was forced onto an elevator. The doors closed with a distinct thud. The button for Floor Three was pushed and within seconds, she was propelled out of the cubicle and into another wide hall. Her guards halted at the fifth door on the left. A plaque on the door stated 312. A key card was waved, and a click sounded. The door swung wide, revealing an apartment-like space.

Lia was shoved in.

Pushing her into an upholstered chair in the small living room, Taz ordered, "Hold out your arm."

Lia spat at him, hugging both arms in tight against her sides, wrapping them around her abdomen. The man swore and then nodded to the guard that must have been a Viking in a previous life. Odin reached out, manhandling Lia's left arm against the arm of the chair. Taz used one hand to hold down both her legs, even as he removed a needle and a vial from his pocket. His helper grinned at her while snapping a piece of rubber tubing in Lia's face, his expression gleeful, before using the tubing as a tourniquet around her upper arm.

Although Lia struggled and yelled, begging them to stop, it was completely ineffectual. Three vials of blood, as well as a half-dozen throat swabs, were taken before the guards ceased their task. At last, one removed the needle, yanked up her right hand, and then pushed her index finger to cover the wound. "Keep it there for about fifteen minutes." He shoved the now filled vials into a pocket before he stood. They walked calmly to the door. The last one to leave, Taz, turned to face her. "Don't leave the room. Don't break anything." His expression hardened. "And don't do anything stupid." His hesitation promised more than his statement. "You wouldn't like the consequences."

It was enough.

Lia succumbed to the fear she'd felt since walking into Stepan's lair, and physically shrank into the chair. Not trusting her voice, she nodded. The relief she felt, when they closed and then locked the door, was immeasurable. Curling her body into a tight ball, the tears began, slowly at first, and then a torrent.

A soft strangled grumbling sound drew her attention. She was alone, so the whimpering had to be from her. The surprise of it was enough to climb out of her pity party.

Taking a deep, calming breath, she turned, taking in the sparseness of the utilitarian room. Taking small, tentative steps, she explored the quarters. It hadn't taken more than fifteen paces to circle the entire apartment. One bedroom, one bath, an efficiency kitchen with only a bar to serve as a dining table. All in all, less than four hundred square feet to house an unwilling guest.

But she knew, this arrangement was, by far, better than Mute's, where ever he was. And no matter what that brother of hers intended, Mute was her first concern.

Her heart ached for him. She'd heard the thud of fist against flesh before the door had closed when they had taken Mute. She knew, from Stepan's harsh statements, along with his obstinate authority, Mute's punishment would be swift, and thorough.

She just hoped thorough didn't mean dead.

Twenty

Mute's battered body endured yet another beating. Sometimes it was one a day, sometimes more. He'd given up counting which one this was. Blow after heavy blow battered his already abused torso. Being strung up, hands tied to a rope attached to the ceiling, stretched up onto his tiptoes, had to be Karma. The significance wasn't lost on him.

He couldn't discern the reason his face was being spared, until the day Lucienne entered the chamber of horrors. Even though revulsion seeped into every cell of his body, the male in him admired the winsome beauty, until he looked into those malevolent eyes. It took monumental effort not to draw back as the back of one long red nail traced his jawline and then the shape of his lips. Somehow, he kept a growl from surfacing.

"For someone who has little interest in Stepan's little sister, the glare you're giving me begs answers, hmmm?" A perfectly arched eyebrow rose, her Parisian accent thick and sensual. "Now why would one such as you want such a trivial…" Full lips pouted, enhancing her accent even further. "And unremarkable little girl? Especially now…" her finger traced down his neck and onto his chest. "Now that you've met me. I can make you forget all about that little chit." Her finger trailed lower, passing his taunt abdomen, heading further south. Her purr deepened as her touch traced the outline of his penis.

Mute didn't breathe. He didn't move. Forcing his mind away from the present, he allowed Lia's face to fill it. Lia's beautiful face was the only thing that mattered. And Lia was ample incentive to keep his attention, and body, in check against Lucienne.

The seductress' fingers closed around him for a brief moment. And then she stepped back, barking orders. "Strip him."

The guard obeyed, unfastening the waistband of his pants and jerking the material to his ankles. The rest had been ripped off long before, too shredded and bloody to be of use anyway.

Focusing on thoughts of Lia, Mute remained still and silent.

Lucienne's breathing increased, the sound mountainous in the tomb-like chamber, as she ran her hand down the length of Mute's back. Fingertips grazed the bruised flesh, following a zig-zag pattern across the breadth of it until they rested lightly at the top of his buttocks. Her gasp was sharp, but as she exhaled, a low, soft moan escaped as her caress lowered. Fingertips stroked solid muscle for long, long moments before she cupped his left buttock in her palm. "Mmmm, my Cherie. You and I are going to be very good together. Yes, very good."

Her other hand snaked around his abdomen and then clamped onto his flaccid shaft.

Mute remained motionless.

"Ah, do I disappoint? Do you find me, um, unappealing?" Her wicked chuckle crooned. "It would disappoint so very much for your appetite to run toward the opposite gender. Hmmm, Cherie?" Her hand lowered, gently caressing his heavy sack for long moments, before making its way again to his broad, muscular chest.

Forcing away thought and reaction wasn't difficult for Mute. He'd had a lifetime of practice. His voice was harsh, full of distaste. "I don't." He finally spared her a disinterested glance. "You're just not worth the effort."

Lucienne tensed into a statue, her face reddening with fury. Those ghastly green eyes fired a god-worthy vehemence at him. And then those long, red nails dug into his chest, dragging down the length of his torso. Red blood sprouted in their trail, all the way to his genitals.

"Continue." She ordered the guard, full lips curled in disgust. Her tone flattened into authoritative indifference. Striking green eyes bore into his. Her deliberate pause was, he knew, meant to intimidate.

"Beat him until he breaks."

Twenty-One

Lia frowned at the smirk on Stepan's face, wondering why she had been summoned. Long days had passed since she had last seen Mute, and as always, he was foremost in her mind. And on her tongue. "Where's Mute? I want to see him. If you've harmed…"

"Your lover is safe." Stepan's eyes darkened. He waved a dismissive hand. "You will see him soon enough." He glanced at the paperwork on his desk for a brief moment before again pinning her with a harsh glare. "But before the reward, one must fulfill the task. It's about time you cooperated, little sister."

"I don't know what you mean." Lia squared slim shoulders, her eyebrows furrowing to match the frown on her lovely face.

"Well, my dear, try as we might, your blood isn't enough." His full lips curved decidedly down. "The code to unlock Father's dream still eludes us."

After the shock of Stepan's revelation abated, Lia laughed, full and deep. The sound filled the room, echoing off the walls. It was particularly pleasant to see Stepan's frown deepen.

"You can have my skin… my hair… my life, I don't care." Lia couldn't help the smirk crossing her lips. "But know this…" she stressed the next word, "*Brother*. I hope you never figure it out."

Stepan stomped to her side. Grasping her hair at the crown, he yanked her head down so their eyes locked. Lia couldn't help a tiny yelp. "Ow."

"Whether we decipher the code today, or the next, nothing is changed. We will find the key. You, nor anyone else, can change that. The world you know will soon be gone." His lips curled into a snarl. "My world, a better world, will take its place."

"Only someone as delusional as you would consider that kind of a world better." Her glare spit fire.

Stepan suddenly released her, throwing his head back and laughing. He laughed until Lia thought he'd gone crazy. But when he finally stopped and again locked stares, she knew the man was way past crazy, having surpassed insanity long ago.

And she knew what she had to do. Tentatively, she placed a light touch on his upper arm. "Brother."

Stepan started, his shocked expression instantly morphing into wariness.

"Stepan. Our father spent his life harnessing the greatest power man has ever known. A power so enormous, most can't even fathom."

Stepan's head jerked at the word *power*.

She'd captured her audience and knew it. Now all she had to do was reel him in. "*Playing* God isn't the objective, is it, Stepan." She paused for effect. "You want to *be* God." Sidling over to stand next to Stepan made her skin crawl, but she managed the necessary steps. "You didn't need my blood, did you? It's not there, is it? Lia smiled slyly and repeated, knowing the effect those two little words would have. "Is it?"

Stepan's handsome face reddened. "Yes. Of course, it is, and I do. It holds the key." His mouth worked, opening and closing as if there were too many words to choose from. His expression jumped from wary and confused to furious in less than a nanosecond as his closed fist pounded the acrylic desk. "You have it, and I want it. I need that key!"

"Why do you need what you already have?"

"But I don't have the sequence, dear sister."

"Yes, you do. You're just too blind to see."

Stepan cocked his head to the left, his eyes narrowing into slits. "No, I don't." It seemed an eternity before either of them breathed. "Onkle ran your DNA through a thousand tests, and the results are always the same." His frown deepened. "It doesn't work."

Lia's back bent slightly, wondering if she was doing the right thing, the best thing for all of mankind. Her whole body tensed, becoming statue-still as the enormity hit her.

But.

Life, as she knew it, would end if she didn't try. Billions would die if she let cowardice rule. "Maybe it's not in the DNA." She prayed she was doing the right thing. "Maybe it's in the prints." She held up her hand.

Just one hand.

Up.

High.

Twenty-Two

Mute could no longer see out of his left eye. It had swollen shut two days ago. Apparently, Lucienne's order to spare his face had been rescinded when he had failed to pleasure her. As much as the woman hated his scathing remarks and his repulsion, he instinctively understood she would have accepted it. What she couldn't tolerate was his indifference to her sensuality. No, Lucienne punished him for not *rising* to the occasion.

And her order to withhold clothing meant her retribution would continue.

The clomp, clomp of boots on concrete signaled the arrival of a visitor. He stiffened at the jingling of keys, followed by the clink of metal hitting metal. A scraping noise declared the door to his cell was opening. Mute rotated his head left to see who had been sent to fetch him. Relief and dread hit him at the same time when Kong entered. Relief, for Kong only followed orders, never embellishing. Dread, for Kong always followed orders, never relenting.

"On your feet." The large man held spacer restraints.

Mute struggled up, holding his side. "What's on the menu today?"

Kong's expression remained impassive, and his tongue stayed silent.

Mute understood, for had their positions been reversed, he, too, would have the same reaction. He frowned. Uneasiness settled in the pit of his stomach. As much as he didn't like it, it would be best to just get this over with. He took a step to the door, for he knew the drill by now. The 'Tank' was the preferred *interrogation room.*

The Tank was large, a good thirty feet by fifty, maybe sixty. It was hard to get an accurate reading when all he saw was fists, clubs, and boots. Still, he welcomed the beatings.

The torture was exactly that.

Pure torture.

"No." Kong held up his empty hand.

Despite years of training, one eyebrow notched up. Mute had to work to erase his quizzical expression.

Another guard stepped into the cell. Mo carried a Taser, and Mute's stomach lurched. They never sent more than one guard to fetch him. It was the only thing going for him. Escape, when the opportunity came, would be through that one guard.

Kong spoke, "Turn around."

Mute hesitated, and Mo started toward him, Taser lifting. Mute complied.

His arms were tugged behind his back. Clamps snapped around each wrist, each held tight and wide, for the spacer bar must have been about eighteen inches. His feet were kicked apart, and then another restraint was clamped onto his ankles.

Mo whined. "Aw man, you could have put up a struggle or something. You know how much I like my toys." The wiry man caressed the black plastic almost reverently.

It was one of the reasons Mute hated Mo. The guard loved gadgets, especially high-electricity, tortuous devices. Another reason was shining in Mo's eyes. The man liked his job.

"You're not my idea of a fun…" Mute stopped mid-sentence. He didn't have to turn around to know another had entered the tiny room. Sniffing the air, the evil in it announced Lucienne's presence far more than the sultry perfume.

"Ah, Cherie, only the foolish forgo the pleasure of *toys.*" Lucienne's silky purr was soft, but the emphasis on her last word was unmistakable. Her tone changed, becoming harsh and commanding. "Leave us."

Mute slowly turned to face the Parisian beauty, his stride clipped by the restraints. Irony slapped him in the face now that he would prefer for Mo to stay.

Mo jeered as he left the room, but the impassivity in Kong hit hard. Until Lia, he, too, had been that dead. The thought of Lia brought a small smile to his lips. He marveled how easy it was to smile now.

Lucienne's eyes widened. Full lips crept up until even white teeth showed. "Ah, Cherie, you are happy to see me, no?" She stepped closer, resting slim fingers atop the hard muscles above his heart.

"Actually, I was thinking of someone else."

Her eyes narrowed before they lowered to follow her hand. "Ah, then I will just have to turn your thoughts to the present." Her fingertips trailed across his bruised torso. "To me."

Mute held still and focused on a crack in the opposite wall. Even that light touch hurt his battered body.

She clucked. "Tsk. Tsk. What a shame to damage such a fine specimen." Looking up from beneath long thick eyelashes, she reached for Mute's chin and forced him to look at her. "There is much pleasure in pain, Mon Cherie."

Mute sucked in a quick breath as her index finger, fitted with an intricately etched gold fingernail-cover bit into his skin. Warm drops trickled down his jaw, and the coppery scent of blood hung in the air.

Lucienne tilted her delicate face, nostrils flaring. An inhuman delight filled her beautiful face while a slight smile pried sensuous lips up, even as her eyes closed. "Mmm…" She brought the tip of the three-inch finger-cover up to her tongue and tasted.

"Delicious." With deliberate movements, the woman placed another identical gold finger-cover on the middle finger of her hand. Stretching out her arm, she wiggled her fingers, obviously admiring the view. Without lifting her face, she looked up at Mute, peering at him from beneath thick, dark lashes.

Knowing the look was calculated did not diminish the effect. The woman had to be one of the most beautiful women on the planet.

Mute remained unaffected. Lia's beauty was unparalleled for it came from strength, goodness, and zest. Wrapping all that inner beauty within the perfection of Lia's outer form and face, well---he had no trouble resisting even such a temptress as the one before him. His lips curled into a cruel sneer. "I don't want to play."

Lucienne's eyes hardened, but her smile lingered, hinting at determination. "Ah, but you will. This is so much better than a beating, is it not? Would you prefer another visit to the Tank? I will recall the guards if that is your wish."

Mute hesitated.

But before he could agree, Lucienne reached up, using the back of her knuckles under his chin, she closed his opening mouth. "See, Cherie, of course, you do not." Self-assurance again filled her expression. Somehow, probably after perfecting the maneuver in a mirror, she smiled and pouted at the same time. Lowering her hand, she let the back of it skim the length of his chest, from his right shoulder all the way to his left hip. "You and I will have much pleasu…" she paused a second, lifting animated, excited eyes to his. "As you say, fun. You will see."

Mute glared at her before returning his attention upon the crack he instinctively knew was going to be a lifeline until this woman left him alone. Stiffening his body, he sealed his lips, remaining silent. He didn't have to look at Lucienne to recognize the anger he'd just instigated.

Suddenly, pain seared, sweeping across his wide chest in the wake of twin trails of red. "Ah, you wound me, Warrior. May I call you Warrior? It suits you." She lifted her hand, and new parallel marks started from his left shoulder, creating a path crossing the previous streaks, ending just below his right hip bone. "Your body is built for it, but more than that. Your *résolu*, ah, tenacity to bring the little chit to her brother reveals more than superior training. Few, if any, could have accomplished such a mission."

There were twelve perfect red X's across Mute's chest, each X marginally lower, for Lucienne had spilled her dissertation slowly. The lowest X ended dangerously close to the top of his outer thigh.

"As much as your skill fascinates, it is not a talent necessary for today's exercise." Her hand lifted abruptly. The point of her gold covered index finger indented the skin two inches below his navel. "The expertise your warrior's body promises is all that is required this day." The metallic nib lowered in a straight line.

Mute tensed when the cold metal pricked the skin above his penis. He forced himself to remain motionless. Still, he couldn't help the soft gasp that escaped when the tip of the nail cover circled the base of his shaft and started a trek along the underside. At least, she wasn't bringing blood, he thought. Mercifully, the pointy tip had vanished. He fought the urge to close his eyes in relief.

However, the compulsion won when Lucienne gripped his balls and squeezed.

Hard.

Stars lit the back of his eyelids, and he bent over with a loud grunt. It took a moment, but he forced his body to straighten. Murder filled his eyes as he turned to glare at his tormentor. "I prefer a soft touch when it comes to foreplay."

Lucienne chuckled throatily. "I do not." Her gaze was meant to mesmerize, and she let it hang between them for several seconds. "And as I am the one…" She laughed at her own joke. "On top, it is I whose preferences will be satisfied." She squeezed again, although with less pressure. "I have every intention of being satisfied."

Although he knew it was futile, he strained against the irons until his jugular threatened to pop. Mute's jaw locked in place. And once again, he sought the solace of the crack on the wall.

"Ah, my Warrior, I am enjoying getting to know you. It is rare for such as you to, um, *visit*. You have an exquisite physique." Lucienne moved behind him. The tip of one nail cover started at the base of his neck, tracing a downward path along his spine. "It has been a long time since I have seen one so…" Her hesitation stretched. "Honed."

Blood dripped delicately, pooling at the rise above his buttocks, before sliding further. Mute shifted when the point continued a straight path. He inhaled sharply when it suddenly veered right.

"Such beauty in a man." The tip lifted as her hand caressed a taut butt-cheek. Her hand moved gracefully back and forth until her fingers curled and two red lines appeared where his thigh met the underside of his buttock.

Mute's teeth clenched.

Lucienne, her fingers slowly trailing, moved to the front of him. Her eyes hardened as her fingers deepened their trek, leaving crimson lines across the entire front of his thigh. A small grunt emerged from behind her smooth lips as, fingers ever-deepening, she slashed the length of his inner thigh.

Mute tensed. There was no doubt his upper thigh sported a crimson necklace of blood. Not for the first time did he wonder if the tips of those damn nail-covers were coated with something to inflict more than the usual pain. Every scrape was on fire, especially his inner thigh, the deepest ones yet.

"Ah, Amoureux. It appears you spoke the truth." She wrapped his flaccid shaft within her fingers.

Thankfully the tips of those nasty covers were pointed away.

Lucienne relaxed. "Maybe you are right, Warrior. Perhaps a tender touch is necessary."

Mute glanced at her and instantly wished he hadn't. Gone was the cruelty, the savagery. In its place was something far more dangerous. Hypnotized, he stared as Lucienne slowly removed first one, and then the other, finger-covers. He returned his focus to the crack. His tense body stiffened.

This time, her touch was feather-light as her hand lowered to his left calf. She bent further until her cheek rubbed against his knee. "Mmmm, you are indeed worthy to be called warrior."

One hand grazed the skin behind his knee, stroking north, and then gently massaged the back of his thigh. "May I make a confession?" She hesitated a moment, fingers held a scant millimeter from his skin. "I have always had a fantasy involving a kilt. You, I think, are the perfect specimen." She traced a path to the front of his knee with all four natural nails. "Next time, though. I am much too impatient today." The temptress leaned into his thigh and kissed it. She pressed dozens of tiny kisses against his leg as she made her way up. He wasn't sure which was worse, the feel of her lips, or her hot breath. Both created goosebumps.

Her light kisses heated Mute's blood. He was, after all, a man. He brought Lia's face to the forefront of his mind, trying to calm the rising fever.

Lucienne's grip tightened against his thigh, her forceful kneading matching the intensity of her ragged breathing. Her other hand leaped to caress behind his other knee as her mouth continued its ascending journey.

Mute chanted within his mind, trying to focus on Lia's beautiful face. *Lia. Lia. Lia.*

Lucienne bit him at the juncture of his abdomen and his left thigh.

Mute gritted his teeth, and began repeating his mantra out loud, the words coarse as sandpaper. "Lia. Lia. Lia."

A throaty chuckle oozed from the woman kneeling in front of him. Her kisses turned into nips as her lips changed course, heading due center. Each nip was healthier than the last. He would have marks for days.

With each bite, his tension strained, until every word strangled, desperate to escape behind clenched teeth.

An oily voice called out from the suddenly opened doorway. "Well, well, I must have Onkle get a sample from you as well. Until now, no one has been able to thwart Lucienne's appetite." Stepan's arms were crossed over his pristine white Charvet dress shirt. "A formula that can keep Lucienne from, how shall I put this, straying… would be priceless." He threw Lucienne a mocking glare.

Lucienne's quick snarl revealed pearl-white teeth sunk deep into the base of Mute's torso. She emitted a low growl, straightened, and then gave both men a murderous glower.

Mute managed to suck in a great amount of air into his parched lungs without showing the pain it caused.

Lucienne slid gracefully to Stepan's side, one hand sliding up the silky cotton on his arm until her body snuggled deeply into Stepan's. "You are my one true love, Mon Amour." She nuzzled his neck, before catching his ear lobe in a tiny nip.

Stepan grunted, pushing her away, his frown formidable. "Find something else to do, Lucienne. I want a word with Worthen."

Lucienne gaped at Stepan for a long minute, before she shrugged daintily.

Mute knew Stepan caught the wink she threw him over her shoulder for Stepan stiffened, his eye's narrowing. He wondered if the bitch was setting him up to endure Stepan's wrath, or if she was warning him of another seduction. Either way, it boded ill.

Stepan waited, studying Mute until Lucienne's soft foot-falls dwindled to nothing. He cleared his throat. "You have a problem."

Mute snorted. "Tell me something I don't know."

Stepan's frown deepened. "Lia has demanded to see you."

Mute forced his expression to remain blank. "That's not an issue for me."

"Yes, it is." The gleam appearing in Stepan's eyes wasn't pretty. "You see, I would like to continue my little game of letting my sister think she has the upper hand by allowing this simple request. And, as such, you will play along."

Mute studied his adversary. "I don't understand."

Stepan shrugged. "Nor are you likely to." He let out a grieved sigh. "She is expecting to find you well, and in, ah, decent shape."

"There's not enough makeup in Hollywood to disguise this kind of abuse." Mute scoffed. "Not to mention a few broken bones." Not only ribs, but fingers, and possibly a wrist, had suffered during his *interrogations*.

"Well, it is what it is."

"What do you want from me?"

Stepan glanced over his shoulder and nodded.

Kong entered the room, carrying a stack of material. He set the bundle on the floor beside Mute's feet. Placing a meaty hand on Mute's bicep, the guard physically turned Mute around.

Mute heard keys jingling and within seconds both ankles were freed. The clamps binding his wrists were removed as well. Mute gently rubbed his swollen wrist with his good hand while doing an about-face. Bending at the waist, he picked up a pair of black cargo pants and began to stuff his legs into them. "How nice of you to do my laundry." Grabbing the charcoal-colored T-shirt, he wondered if he could get it up, over his head, and on without crying out. He would be damned if he would allow Stepan to see his pain. Gritting his teeth, he started lifting the shirt.

"Please. There is tape to wrap your torso." Stepan locked gazes with Mute, his tone belligerent.

"We don't want Lia to think you have been mistreated."

He was going to see Lia. That's all that mattered right now. A smile surfaced, both on his face and in his heart. He was going to see Lia. The thought of Lia kept the pain at bay while Kong wrapped his ribs.

Stepan's cruel laugh shattered the jubilation. "If you decide to *elaborate* the details of your incarceration and Lia refuses to cooperate with Onkle and me, then…" He paused as if searching for the correct words. "I will have no use for her. Alive, that is." His chin ducked a fraction and his sinister gaze intensified. "Her body will be donated to science. Mine." He paused. "Are we clear?"

Mute snarled the word through gritted teeth. "Crystal."

Stepan's tight stance loosened. "Good." He waved a hand at Kong, who was handing Mute two towels, one wet, and the other dry. "Please wash and then finish dressing. I will have Lia summoned." He started for the door, but stopped, facing Mute once more. "Lucienne has little experience with either rejection or denial. And her claws are sharp." His gaze landed on the red scratches visible above and below the tape covering Mute's chest. "It may be that her vengeance will turn in another direction." Stepan shrugged a shoulder. "For Lia's sake, I hope not."

Mute's heart contracted and ice filled his blood, a shiver involuntarily running down the length of his spine. No doubt Stepan's assessment was correct. He had to warn Lia. Finishing his so-called bath, he slipped on the T-shirt. His grimace was mild compared to what it could have been. The rigidity of the tape helped with the pain. Even so, it took a moment to catch his breath.

When he could do so, Mute shot Kong a critical glare. "You can leave anytime. I don't need you to hold my hand."

"My orders are to stay." The guard's countenance remained emotionless.

Mute's heart sank. He should have guessed he would not be left alone with Lia. What was surprising was that they were not meeting in a monitored area.

The silence in the room grew tangible as they waited for Lia's arrival. Mute began to pace. At long last, boots could be heard in the corridor. He broke for the door. Kong stepped into his path, but it didn't matter.

Lia shot through the opening. "Mute?" Her gaze searched first right and then left, hunting for him. The relief flooding her face when their eyes met overjoyed him.

Mute leaped for her, as she ran to him. It was all he could do to hold a groan in check when she landed against his ribs. But it didn't matter. He crushed her against him, not caring about the pain. "Lia." Every sentiment overwhelming him---love, joy, relief, and horror permeated not only in his voice but every pore in his body. He wrapped his arms around her, wanting to pull her inside his skin.

Lia shook in his arms. The sound of her sobs filled the room. She held on to him as tightly as he did her. It was enough, for the moment. Finally, Lia inched back and gazed up, pale cheeks streaked with tears.

Mute sighed and released his bear-like grip, although still locking her against him with one arm. Reaching out, he tenderly swiped his thumb across her cheeks, wiping away the moisture. When the tears continued to fall, he bent slightly and kissed them away. Her face heated under his touch and, as if magnetic, her lips called his.

Her lips were sweet, already parted, and hungry when he bent, capturing their sweetness with his own possessive lips.

A fire blazed within him at her response and his gentle caress deepened. Tilting his head for a better angle, he captured her head within both hands and ravished her lips. Her soft, low moan drove the fire coursing through his blood into white-hot magma. Her hands separated, one trailing a path around his waist, the other sneaking up to the back of his neck. He loved the feel of her fingers digging into his scalp, pulling his head closer.

He groaned, the sound long and deep.

"Ahem." Kong coughed, using a fist to cover his mouth.

Lia started, her body trembling before she pulled away. Her arms dropped, and she stepped back.

Mute let her go, wondering if her shivers were from his kiss or Kong's interruption. Still, he liked how their lips were the last to disentangle, enough that a grin teased his mouth before he shot Kong a decidedly thunderous look.

It gave Lia adequate time to recover. "Oh, Mute." Her amber eyes swept over him, worry filling them as they traveled over the assorted cuts and bruises.

Mute smiled at her concern and shook his head. "I'm fine, sweetheart. Shhh. There's nothing to worry about. You're here, that's all that matters."

"But…"

Mute pulled her head into the pocket between his shoulder and his breast, stroking her hair. "I'm fine, really." Absolutely fantastic now that he could hold her, touch her, and know she was unharmed.

Lia's eyes filled, and one hand lifted to his face, caressing his cheek.

Mute leaned into her palm. His eyes closed, and his breathing deepened. If only he could capture this moment and stamp it into his heart, holding it for all time. He would give anything to own this memory forever.

Eventually Lia stirred, pulling back against his arms, and glanced up at him. The tears had dried, but the tracks were still visible on her cheeks. "Oh, Mute. I'm so sorry you're involved in this. Stepan only wants me. Or rather, my DNA. He doesn't need you anymore, but…"

Mute placed a finger over her moving lips. "Shhh. This is why I was born."

Lia's brows puckered. "Huh?"

A slight, knowing smile crossed his face as the truth sank home. "You once asked where I was born, and I told you Michigan. Detroit, to be specific." His finger moved, along with his hand, and stroked her shoulder, flowing down her back. "What I didn't tell you was how I grew up on the streets and then joined the army at fourteen." At the shock on her face, he continued. "I looked twenty. The streets will do that to you."

"Oh, Mute. Was it awful?"

He shrugged. "It made me who I am."

Her arms tightened and her head, once again, lay on his shoulder. "Didn't you have anyone to nurture you? Help you grow? Anyone?"

"My third set of foster parents was an elderly widow, but she cared. I stayed with her until she died. I was eight." He shrugged. "When they placed me with a guy who liked using his fists, I ran away." His hesitation wasn't intentional. "The streets taught me how to survive. Something you and I need right now."

Abruptly he locked anxious eyes with hers and gripped her shoulders so hard she absently winced, but he didn't let up. If anything, his stare intensified. "You will survive. Everything you do from this point on is centered on your survival. Get it?" When she didn't answer, he gently shook her and asked again. "Do you hear me? Do you understand?"

Lia appeared transfixed, until that last shake. And then she let out a huge breath. "Yes, I understand."

Mute pulled her tight against his body, loving the warm softness of her curves. A small sigh escaped him. "You must live. You have to." He shifted so he could stare into her eyes. "You have to do anything to survive. Do you hear?"

A tear trickled out of her right eye. And then another slipped from her left. Delicate brows knotted above her nose and her chin quivered. "Oh, Mute. I'm so sorry." She grasped for his hands as a great sob shook her body. "So sorry."

He smiled down at her. "Don't be. I know now why I was born. And why my upbringing wasn't more sheltered." A grin flashed before it vanished, swallowed by seriousness. "I was born to save you, Lia. My whole life has been a training ground for…" he waved his hand at the cell surrounding them. "Now."

"But…

"You're worth it." Framing her face within his rough hands, he repeated, voice concrete hard. "Lia, you're worth it all, everything. I would gladly endure everything again, twice as much, knowing my background, my training is the reason I can save you. You are so worth it, worth it all." Seizing her supple lips with his own, proving, beyond the shadow of a doubt, he meant every word.

Lia melted in his arms, her body sinking into his.

Mute's hands traveled over her back as the depth of his love poured from ravenous lips. They caressed supple hips, one perfect behind, sneaking up tantalizing curves before again catching her face between rough hands. Ultimately, he had to surface for air.

Mute pressed his forehead onto hers as he gulped in oxygen. It took several moments before he could speak. "My life's goal is to save you, Lia. It's taken until now to know it, but it's the truth. Every part of my life conditioned me for now. Right now. To save you."

Lia lifted her face, locking brimming, shining eyes to his. "You've got the now right." Her face hardened into determination. One hand dropped from his back and reached into her pocket. "It's time, Mute."

Twenty-Three

Mute watched, transfixed, as Lia jumped at Kong, plunging a syringe into the guard's neck. His own eyes mirrored Kong's as the minion's eyes filled with disbelief. Incredulity mounted further as Lia batted at the suddenly uncoordinated defenses Kong valiantly attempted. Astonishment knocked him for a loop as he watched Kong disintegrate into a pool of mush, the shock in the man's wide eyes echoing his own before they closed in a drug-fogged sleep. For a moment, Lia stood over her inert prey.

And then those intense amber orbs sought his.

Mute shook his head as if to clear it. He barely heard her rushed words.

"We're getting out of here. Now. Are you coming?" Lia grabbed for his hand, gripping tight and pulling hard.

Mute allowed her to lead him from the cell, wondering what the end result of Lia's rescue attempt would be. Speculation turned to amazement when she stopped, jerking him up short. His shock magnified when she snatched an object, something fabric, from a pocket and chunked it at a camera. They waited as it soared toward the mounted lens, and before it could fall to the ground, Lia tugged him across the line-of-view.

"There's only two more," Lia shouted over her shoulder as she ran ahead, pulling him behind her.

Mute stumbled to keep up, especially when she spun a hard ninety and sprinted for the next exit. Wrapping an arm around his waist, he ignored the pain from his ribs. Their intertwined hands kept her within arm's length, and a realization hit---he was slowing her down.

A coldness settled over his entire body, the intensity almost freezing him in place. He stopped dead in their tracks. "Go." His brows furrowed, his gaze searching the heavens, before sucking in a great breath as his eyes found the floor. "Go now. Save yourself. I'm only slowing you down."

Lia turned, eyes frantic, those succulent lips forming an open o. "No. I'm not leaving without you, Mute." She tugged on his hand, pulling with all her might. When he didn't budge, she threw a dangerous look in his direction. "Look, Snow-flake. We are getting out of here if I have to drag your enormous butt behind me. I may look like a cream puff, but just try me." Her eyebrows knotted and her luscious lips thinned to a single straight line. "I'm getting the hell out of here, and you're coming with me. Anything about that you don't understand?"

Mute decided silence was the best option and remained true to his name.

He nodded.

Lia nodded back, the determination in her eyes somehow softening and hardening at the same time. "Good. Then let's get the hell out of here." She turned, leading him through a couple of passages and up a set of stairs. Halting at a closed door, she turned to him, holding an index finger against her lips, motioning him into silence.

He nodded.

Lia pressed one ear against the door, her eyebrows furrowed, lips flattened and tight.

Seconds passed while Mute fought the impulse to take charge.

Although trained and admittedly an expert in exactly this kind of scenario, he knew Lia was smart, and so far, her plan was working. He was man enough to acknowledge her expertise at the moment.

Her voice was hushed, tight. Her body remained ready to spring. "Two guards are on the other side of this door. If we time it correctly, we can catch them together, right outside… the…"

Lia leaped, and Mute followed, already knowing what was necessary. Lia took out the first guard with a sweep of her left foot. Mute overpowered, and then snapped the neck of the second guard a half-a-second behind. And then he cold-cocked the first guard Lia had knock off-balance. The man would be out for hours.

Lia reached for his hand, dragging him away from the downed guards.

Mute sprinted to keep up. One last look at the carnage behind him reinforced the knowledge Lia had a script and he better not screw it up.

He stepped it up, doing double-time, and managed to stay by her side as they raced up the stairs, opting not to take the elevator. They reached the main level in under a minute.

Fear crinkled her brows when she slowed at the door facing them. The look she threw him shouted dread and uncertainty.

Mute understood.

It was time for him to take charge. Without hesitation, he took a purposeful step forward, his hand reaching for the door handle.

"What are you doing?" Her whisper hit his ears with the force of a typhoon. And then she grabbed his hand and swung him behind her body. "Stop. I have to count."

When her lips mouthed the number five, she peered up at him and gave a slight nod. "Now." Lia opened the door a crack, neck craning to see around the metal structure, and into the hall. "Clear." She tossed him a determined look and then tugged on his hand as she eased into the passage. "Hurry. We've only seconds."

Mute did as he was told. But doubt was a powerful entity. "How do you plan on getting past the six guards watching the main floor?"

Lia didn't slow, pitching the words over a slim shoulder. "That's your specialty, not mine." Her breathing hitched. "And goons one and two are up...now."

Mute's open mouth threatened to slow his attack as two men appeared from nowhere, racing toward them. Instantly, training took over and before his heart beat twice, both men lay unconscious on the tile floor.

Lia lunged forward, jumping over the downed men. "Only four to go."

Mute followed, pumping his legs to keep up.

A door loomed, and Lia lunged for it. Stopping for a half of one heartbeat, she faced him, trepidation written all over her. An outstretched hand clasped the door handle, but she didn't open it.

Scanning his face instead, it appeared she waited until some sort of answer was gained from his expression.

Every instinct said go. He hoped his expression did as well even though silence was his usual norm.

Lia's questioning gaze hardened and she gave him a stiff nod. Abruptly, she sprang for the handle and yanked the door open.

Two guards lunged through the opening, and Lia sprang backward.

Mute, understanding her silent command, rushed forward. Surprise registered on both men's faces as he simultaneously used his fists as battering rams. His right cross and a matching left cross slammed into each man's jaw at the same time. His reward was two sets of eyes rolling back in their heads before they slumped to the floor.

He threw Lia a *What's Next* inquiry before running full out beside her, holding his ribs in place as best he could

Lia ran, and he followed. Down passageways, and up floors. He took out the guards on two levels, and then she dragged him down the last corridor. Lia stiffened. "Here. Five guards. Each patrolling a section."

Mute tensed, ready to attack.

Suddenly, Lia stiffened. And then her face went polar white.

Full lips thinned until they almost disappeared. Her brow wrinkled to the point her huge eyes squinted to half their usual size. She snaked a hand to his upper arm and pulled. "Wait."

Mute did.

For long silent moments.

He could read the hesitancy crossing her face. A part of him hated when she made the decision. All they had to do was get past this door, and they would be home free. Free.

He sighed.

Free, for how long?

Lia was right. They had to go back.

Her tone wavered between regret and determination. "I can't leave them."

"Who?" He was pretty sure they each had different reasons why they couldn't leave yet.

"The people Stepan is using for his experiments. The people he's kidnapped." Frustration filled her face. "We don't have time for this."

Mute stilled. "Where are they? And how many?"

"I'm not sure how many, but there's..." Lia's voice lowered. "Several. And all are on the third floor. Stepan keeps us all..." her intonation turned bitter. "Ready." She stiffened. "I have to help them. It's only because of them I know how to get us out of here."

Mute nodded, looking at a set of stairs behind Lia. "You go. It should be clear now. The guards will be out for hours."

Lia reached for his hand. "Not without you."

He knew what had to be done. "You free the captives. I'll destroy the weapon." He squeezed the hand holding him in place. "And kill Stepan." He rushed on. "I'm sorry, but your brother can't live. He will never stop hunting you or trying to rule the world. Even destroying what he's created will only be

a set-back. In time, he would re-create everything."
He hated the pasty white her face had turned. "I have
to do this, Lia. It's not optional."

Lia's shaking head slowly started to nod, and
some of the color returned to her face. "Yes, I
understand Stepan cannot be allowed to live. But, we
don't have time to take out the weapon. And it's not
necessary. Without Stepan or me, it can't work."

He wasn't sure if it was the calculation or the
resolve in Lia's eyes that made him dread what she
was about to say.

"Come. We'll free the prisoners, and use their
distraction to take out Stepan." She tugged on his
hand as she took a purposeful step toward the stairs.
"But we're going to do this together."

Mute sighed and then followed. They had run
out of time. Besides, her plan had merit. "Okay,
where on the third floor?"

Lia called over her shoulder, never slowing
down. "All of it."

Mute scowled. At the stairwell landing, he
pushed in front of Lia, reaching for the door handle.
He stopped all movement and held his breath.

Lia whispered softly as she, too, halted.
"There shouldn't be any more guards." She tried to
slip around him.

Mute remained still, blocking her path. "I'll
check the corridor. You wait until I give the all-
clear." When annoyance began to fill her eyes, he
repeated, harsh enough to make it an order. "Not
before. Got it?"

Lia nodded, her body relaxing slightly. "Got
it."

Mute silently opened the door a crack, listening.

Nothing.

Slipping through the door, he hesitated. The long corridor promised at least twenty doors on each side. His stomach dropped. That's a lot of people. Far more than he'd expected. He cursed silently before opening the door wider, allowing Lia to enter the hall. Motioning for her to remain silent, he gestured her to start at the opposite side and, following his example, try to open the closest door.

Of course, it was locked.

Mute stood helpless and dumbfounded when Lia threw him an exasperated look before she sprinted down the hall and retrieved a key-card hanging from a hook beside the main entrance. He wanted to slap his head and had mentally done so by the time she returned to his side.

Her grin was infectious, and he returned it with one of his own when she passed the card over a metal panel beside the door. A click sounded, and Mute turned the knob. The door opened easily.

A man dressed in khakis pants and a cotton shirt stood just inside the door. Behind wire-rimmed glasses, his eyes widened. Mute quickly put a finger to his lips, nodding.

The man nodded back.

Mute crooked a finger and gestured for the man to follow.

He did.

Mute and Lia repeated the process over and over. Until the corridor filled with people and every door had been unlocked. Thankfully, over half of the rooms had been empty, but that still left eighteen extras Mute had to see to safety.

By now, it would be inconceivable for Stepan to be unaware of their escape attempt. No matter. He was next on the list. All Mute had to do was get these people to the main factory, and the workers there could get them to the outside. Stepan could covertly command a lot of people, but not the hundreds employed in the main factory. A secret of Stepan's magnitude would have leaked long ago.

When they reached the end of the hallway and were faced with a choice of direction, Mute asked softly, "Anyone know the way to the main work area?"

A middle-aged woman in sensible shoes spoke up. "Yes, most everyone uses the common passages, but since I used to report directly to Mr. Kovolev..." Abruptly, a shiver raced through the woman, hard enough that her voice quit working mid-stream. She swallowed and then continued, "There is a back way. I used it all the time before my imprisonment."

Several grunts and head-nods of sympathy passed through the crowd.

"Is it isolated?" Mute asked.

The woman nodded.

"Where is it?"

"Just to the right of the elevator, there is a door marked 'Authorized Personnel Only'. The stairs lead straight to the main floor, and it is only two doors down from the main work area."

Turning to the first to be rescued, Mute asked, "Can you get these people there?"

The man in khaki nodded. Mute believed him for the eyes behind the glasses narrowed with determination. Reaching out his hand, he smiled. "Good, then go. All of you go."

The man shook Mute's hand, clasping his other hand on top of Mute's and with both pumped hard. "Thank you. Thank you so much."

Lia tugged on Mute's forearm, her hand bouncing from the force of the handshake. "Mute, we've got to go."

The man nodded but continued to pump. "Thank you, Mute."

Mute released his grip, reached for Lia's arm, and spun, calling over his shoulder as the pair sprinted down the hallway. "Go. Now."

Lia ran flat out beside him. "Where do you think Stepan is?"

Mute had no idea. "We'll find him. We have to."

Lia gasped for breath. "What about his office?"

"Do you remember how to get there?"

"Not really."

They stopped. They had to make a directional choice. Mute headed them up. "If I were him, I'd be where I could watch over my masterpiece."

Lia raced up the stairs, one step behind him. "You're probably right."

The top landing was in sight. Only three more steps to reach it.

Lia pulled hard, stopping their forward momentum. "Mute, I didn't expect to face Stepan.

My only concern was getting us out of here. I haven't got a plan for this."

Mute smiled wide, showing tons of white. The enormity of it surprised him, and apparently, Lia, by her wide-eyed response. Pulling her into his strong arms, he rested his cheek on her hair, loving the smell of her, the warmth of her, the softness of her, and everything else about her. "There's only one plan, Lia. The one saving you…" He paused. "For me."

Lia visibly softened, sinking into him, wrapping her arms around him. For a moment, all was right in the world.

"Ah, there you are." A caustic voice hung in the air.

Mute tensed.

Lia cringed.

"If my guess is correct, you are looking for me? Hmmm?" Stepan's cryptic voice promised torment.

Mute let his arms drop before spinning to face Stepan. The sight of the weapon made his blood freeze. Nonchalance filled every cell for he'd had years of practice. "Good guess. We were. It would have been rude not to say goodbye."

Stepan's laugh was more of a bark. He gestured with the weapon, waving it toward the door. "Yes. But then again, it is rude to leave when my invitation is still, shall we say, open."

Mute moved to take the lead and finish the climb.

"No. Lia first."

When Mute hesitated, the direction of Stepan's weapon changed. It no longer pointed at him. Instead, Lia became the target.

Stepan's left eyebrow rose as he waited.

Lia nudged Mute to the side and took the last few steps leading to the fifth floor.

Kong held the door open for them. The usually dispassionate Kong's face was red and sported a bruise the length of forehead to jaw. Apparently, Stepan's anger had got the better of the big man's face. Fury pulsed through Kong and Mute recognized going through this man was going to be punishing. He met Kong's stare with a determined glare of his own. One of them wasn't going to survive the day, and they both knew it.

Stepan's tone returned to conversational. "I was willing to wait for you in my office. However, waiting is boring. And you were taking so long." He gestured for Kong to lead the way. "I had no doubt you would come for me. Even you would realize I could never let Lia go." As if an afterthought, he added. "She is my sister, after all."

Kong opened the office door, standing at attention until Stepan motioned for him to enter the room behind the trio.

"Ah, Mon Ame. You've returned." Lucienne spun the chair she was sitting in, to face the arrivals. A cruel smile curved her sensuous mouth. Long legs were crossed, one foot bouncing in the air to an inaudible beat, black silk-covered forearms resting on the armrest, while long nails tapped in time with her foot.

Mute's chilled blood heated with anger, but he kept the emotion hidden.

Lucienne stretched slowly, the movement graceful and seductive. Stealthily, she crossed the room to stand in front of Mute. Her almond eyes raked him from head to toe, and her smile softened. "I'm so glad you couldn't leave." She threw a quick glance at Lia, who stood to the side, before again settling her gaze on Mute. There was a calculated gleam behind the fire in them. She let her hand trail lazily over Mute's broad chest. "I've so enjoyed our little…trysts. It is difficult to find such a fulfilling lover, no?"

Lia's gasp could have been heard on the moon.

Lucienne's smile widened as she snagged Lia's eyes. "Ah, little one. You did not know? Or is it that you do not know how, um, pleasing?"

Mute swatted away Lucienne's hand. "Don't."

"Ah, my Warrior. Surely, you don't deny the pleasure of this?" Lucienne held up her right hand, wiggling her fingers. The index and middle finger were fitted with the gold nail-covers.

"Lucienne, I haven't the time or the desire to play your little games." Stepan crossed the room in two steps and yanked on Lucienne's hand, stripping off the nail covers. They clattered loudly on the tile.

Lucienne huffed, her lips forming a beautiful pout. "Please, Stepan…"

Stepan's posture tightened, and his voice rose. "Not now, Lucienne. You can either be silent, or you can leave." He waved a hand toward the chair she had so recently vacated. "It's your choice, my dear."

Silently, Lucienne, arms crossed over her chest, retrieved her nail-covers before stalking to the chair and sinking into it.

Mute could only see one way out of this.

He had no weapons, no help, and no plan.

All he had was what had kept him alive for thirty-three years, an overwhelming desire to survive. Focusing on his sole task of saving Lia, Mute realized there wasn't going to be any opportunities. He was going to have to create his own.

It came when Stepan turned his back on them when the man started to amble back to his desk. Mute leaped, jumping on Stepan. He knifed the side of his hand hard against Stepan's unprotected neck. Stepan's cry of surprise cut off mid-yell.

Lucienne, caught off guard by the attack, hesitated too long.

Mute's attention centered on Kong, who had instantly jumped to defend his employer.

Mute dropped to Stepan's unconscious body, reaching for the weapon that had fallen out of Stepan's hand. His fingers closed around it. Pointing it at Kong, he pressed against the indentation that was positioned where a trigger should be.

Nothing happened.

Kong batted it away from Mute's grip and then smashed a right cross against Mute's cheek. Blood splattered them both as previous cuts and gashes reopened.

It staggered Mute for a millisecond, and he caught a glimpse of Lia and Lucienne grappling.

Kong had to die.

And he had to do it as quickly as possible.

Kong threw a heavy left and Mute stepped into it, taking the punishing wallop. It would not have been his first choice, but he had to hurry. Lia needed him. His eyes watered from the pain. Blinking rapidly, he charged into Kong, body-slamming him into the wall. Before Kong could react, Mute pounded an elbow into Kong's damaged face.

Kong roared and then bucked, his eyes wild, trying to dislodge Mute's hold.

Mute growled, the deep rumbling pulsing up from his core. During the time it took for the sound to escape from behind clenched teeth, Mute had wrapped both arms around Kong, squeezing hard enough to pinch vertebra.

Kong resisted, desperately trying to raise his arms.

Mute saw the head-butt coming but got one in first.

Kong's head banged against the wall with such force the man's body jerked and relaxed fully, if only for a second.

Mute took full advantage, and squeezed harder, inching the man toward the door. Several hooks, probably for hanging lab coats, protruded there, and would be an effective weapon if he could just get Kong into position.

Kong tried to bring his arms together, obviously hoping the open space would allow him to slip out of Mute's grip.

Mute was ready for the maneuver and used it, hauling Kong's body toward the hooks. The way the man didn't resist informed Mute Kong hadn't guessed why, yet. Realization hit Kong too late when Mute was able to wrangle the man where he wanted him.

Kong again struggled violently, but Mute held him in place and then delivered a violent head-butt to his opponent.

Kong went limp, his intense glare slowly dimming.

Mute sighed and then relaxed his hold, letting the lifeless Kong slip to the floor. Blood trailed down the wall, along with a deep scratch from the broken hook sticking out from the back of Kong's head.

The grunts and punches sounded loud now that something other than Kong centered his attention. Mute spun, finding Lucienne kicking Lia's left shoulder in a martial arts maneuver that would make Jackie Chan proud.

Lia looked about all done in. Her face sported bruising that would soon darken. Her shirt was ripped, and a dark red stain was visible on the front. Her lip was cut and bleeding.

Anger fired Mute, and he charged at Lucienne.

Lucienne saw him coming and, pushing against Lia for momentum, lunged for him while bending back, letting a stiff-arm sweep at his ankles, bringing him down. Before he could recover, she kicked his battered ribs, not once, but twice.

His groan was almost loud enough to wake the dead.

Lucienne smiled. It was not pretty.

She circled Mute as he struggled up. "Ah, Mon Cherie. Does it surprise you that I am also quite skilled in other areas?" Her cruel smile widened.

Mute, rising stiffly, began to grumble, the sound guttural and growing. He, too, began to move in a circle, matching Lucienne's every step.

Lucienne made several quick kicks, each hitting Mute in a damaged area, but she didn't press the advantage. Mute wondered if she thought to wear him down before she went for the kill.

It didn't matter. His death wasn't on his agenda. Hers was.

A sudden thought occurred to him, and he glanced at Lia. His inattention was rewarded with two quick successive kicks to the ribs. He grabbed a cautious breath, but his gaze remained on Lia.

It was as if her voice looped a recording in his head. *Real men don't hit women. Real men don't hit women.* He absorbed a kick to the jaw. *Real men don't hit women.*

Lucienne wore an expectant look, although there was no hesitation when she struck again, a hard, straight-legged kick to the ribs, followed by another. She bounced to a standstill, hands clenched in front of her, half raised in a defensive posture.

Mute remained still, his stance as stiff as his expression.

Lucienne's head tilted to the side. The puzzlement in her beautiful face morphed into understanding. Her hands dropped to her sides as her body straightened, completely vulnerable. "Ah, Mon Ame? So honorable. You are truly a rare specimen. How refreshing to find a man who will not harm the fairer sex."

Lia, tense and expectant, hollered up at him from where she had collapsed on the floor. "What are you waiting for?"

Something on his face must have revealed his dilemma. Or maybe it was the quick glance he threw at her temple.

Understanding hit like a spotlight and Lia's eyes hardened. She spat out the words. "That one's not a woman. She's a... a...Demon." Lia screamed at the top of her lungs. "Get her!"

Lucienne was spewing the rest of her dissertation to Mute, oblivious to his and Lia's discourse. "Or is it because of all we have shared, Cheri? I do hope that…"

Mute stepped into the punch, the momentum adding to the force. It caught Lucienne on her mouth, splitting it, just like Lia's. Lucienne's eyes rolled back into their sockets, as her body slumped and fell.

He should catch her. He didn't want to. At the last possible moment, he did it anyway. Just enough that Lucienne didn't break anything when she hit the ground with a small thud.

Lia smiled weakly at him as she struggled to rise. He reached her side before her next breath and wrapped her within the sanctuary of his arms. Lia jerked at the contact of his chest against her face, but immediately relaxed, wrapping her own arms around his waist.

Mute squeezed Lia in close, his nostrils filling with her sweet, womanly scent for several long moments, grateful she was his once again.

He recognized his mistake one second too late.

A scrape sounded, and Mute knew in that moment, only Lia was going to survive today. Thrusting her behind him, he rotated a full one-eighty, facing Stepan.

Stepan appeared bent as if he couldn't get his body to fully straighten. But the weapon in his hand was rock steady. His expression wasn't angry, only mildly curious. "Did you try to use this?" He held the weapon slightly higher. The metal object was too round to be an actual gun. Still, it boasted a barrel and a grip.

Mute nodded, wondering why this was important.

Stepan nodded. "That's good. Then the imprinting worked."

Mute understood. The weapon wouldn't allow anyone but Stepan to fire it. The concept was a sound one. It offered protection against anyone stripping the weapon and shooting the owner.

And Stepan's interest would buy him time. Hopefully enough to save Lia.

"What is it?" Mute raised his eyebrows before glancing at the weapon.

"The technical name is Velsic 426. But now that I know it works, I'll have to come up with a marketable name." Stepan took a step back, resting his rear on the desk. "Any suggestions?"

Lia shoved at Mute. Caught off-guard, he was easily pushed to the side.

"Yeah," Lia said. "How about 'Stick it up your…'"

Mute again stepped in front of Lia. "Actually, I was thinking of something entirely different."

Crimson began to creep up Stepan's neck, settling onto his cheeks. "Now, now, dear sister. There's no need for that." Stepan straightened, rising off the desk. A steely glint hardened his gaze. "At least your death will prove valuable. I think it fitting you both will have the honor of demonstrating what this weapon can do." He waved the weapon at Mute, indicating the pair needed to exit the room.

Mute let his hand grip Lia's arm as if to guide her. Instead, he jerked her back, and down, leaping toward Stepan at the same time. Stepan's eyes rounded, as did his mouth.

The weapon fired.

A laser grazed Mute's left arm before it cut a black path across the wall and up onto the ceiling, for he'd been able to shove Stepan's aim to the side. He winced but did not slow down.

A high-pitched whine filled the air, and Stepan's frantic glance at the weapon told the truth well enough for Mute to grasp. The weapon had to recharge before it could fire again.

A mirthless smile tilted Mute's lips as he clasped Stepan's arms within his huge hands. All he had to do now was break the man's neck, and they'd be…

A shout, and then yelling, along with the sounds of running feet and furniture scraping across the tile floor filled the air. Men, in uniform, poured through the doorframe. Behind them, the man in Khaki and the woman in sensible shoes entered the room.

Mute remained still as two uniforms pried his hands off his prisoner. They slapped one of Stepan's

wrists into handcuffs and struggled to get his other
hand entrapped.

Stepan bellowed and lunged from their grip,
grabbing for the weapon Mute had knocked to the
floor. Again, Mute leaped for Stepan.

So did Lia, her face a mask of resolve.

Lia got there first, yelling, "No, Stepan!"

Suddenly, the laser went off, the light of it
trapped between Stepan and Lia.

Mute roared, lunging to pull them apart.
"No!"

Time stopped.

A lifetime of seconds passed.

Stepan's eyes locked with Lia's, his lips
lifting into a sad little smile. "My dear sister. We
could have been so good together."

The world froze for several long heartbeats.

Mute's heart stopped as both Stepan and Lia's
expressions morphed from shock to horror.

And then, their bodies entangled, both Stepan
and Lia slipped, inch by precious inch, to the floor.

Stepan's intense gaze on Lia slowly
disintegrated into blankness, his eyes becoming
clouded and unfocused.

Lia, her face pinched with both fear and
disgust, jerkily fought against Stepan's dead weight
as her brother slumped to the ground.

Mute reached for her, drawing Lia up and
holding her out for inspection. When there didn't
appear to be a new red spot growing anywhere on her
torso, he sighed heavily with relief and pulled her into
his embrace. "Woman…" He began to rant at her, but

couldn't. Mute had to fight just to breathe. Pulling in lungfuls of air interfered with his ability to speak.

The weapon slipped from Lia's numb fingers. Tears filled her eyes as she peered into Mute's empathetic ones. "I didn't want…" She swallowed hard. "I couldn't let him shoot you." Goosebumps popped up all over her skin. "I wasn't trying to kill him."

Mute ran a shaking hand down her hair. "Shhh. Hush now. I know you didn't."

Lia lifted her face, tear tracks fresh on her cheeks. "Really, I was only trying to stop you from being hurt, or killed."

"I know, sweetheart. I know." He continued to stroke her hair. "I know. Now shhh."

Mute refused to let Lia go. While the authorities questioned him and even when his saviors tried to explain the rescue, he held her tight within his arms.

Enri Van Houten, wearing khakis and a cotton button-down, explained that, although Kovolev's henchmen tried to apprehend the escapees, some got away, he included, along with Mrs. Gorchevsky, the woman in the sensible shoes. They'd wasted no time in contacting the police. Even though it was evident no one believed Billionaire Stepan Kovolev, owner of the largest gun manufacturer in the world, would stoop to criminal activities, the authorities felt obligated to check it out.

When the factory proved to be everything Van Houten and Gorchevsky promised, they had no choice but to call in the manpower to take over Kovolev's building.

Most of Kovolev's thugs were still unconscious, making capture a breeze. Others only delayed the process of rounding up Kovolev's hirelings. It was only when a uniform lifted Kong's body, looking for weapons, Mute remembered Lucienne.

Frantically, he looked around.

Lia, still clamped within his frame, glanced up.

"I don't see Lucienne," Mute said.

She stiffened, searching the room. "Neither do I. Where is she?"

Mute's frown turned into a scowl. "Probably long gone from here. No doubt, she slipped out during the commotion."

Lia's voice dropped to a whisper. "Do you think they will ever catch her?"

"Of course," Mute lied.

He prayed the lie would come true.

Twenty-Four

Two days later, Lia reclined on a comfortable seat in an SV carriage bound for Germany, dealing with too much turmoil to succumb to the hypnotic clackity, clack, clack of the wheels. Although she'd wanted to leave Moscow immediately, the authorities refused her application for a transit visa. At least until they were finished with her.

It took a full day.

And waiting for the proper travel documents ate up the next, dictating the utilization of the last train out of Moscow. They should arrive in Berlin tomorrow morning.

A frown played on her face, and it had nothing to do with the faint odor of steel and fumes blended with the spicy aroma from the kitchen car. She tried to concentrate on the hint of aseptic air freshener wafting from the ventilation ducts. Mixed all together, the scent wasn't unpleasant, it only reminding her of where she was.

And why.

The reason was sitting across from her, looking far too gorgeous for her piece of mind. Folding her arms across her chest, she frowned, turning to Mute. "I know you think I need an escort, but I don't. I can get back to the States without your help." Lia wasn't sure she wanted his help. Or his company.

The thunderstorm in his eyes suggested she better change her mind, but before she could protest, the scowl vanished, sorrow replacing it. His voice was husky and deep, filled with regret. "You don't need anything from me. I know you are capable of making your way home." His gaze dropped to the floor. "I'm the one who needs you."

Lia didn't answer, taking the time to study the mercenary in front of her. He was still huge and a mass of muscles. His focus now seemed to be centered on remaining attached at her hip. But the sharpness in those dark eyes was gone, as was the assurance.

It was hard to believe this was the same man who had captured her what seemed ages ago. Vulnerability weighed uneasily on his shoulders. It filled his eyes every time he looked at her.

And that seemed to be every other second.

Every time she caught his stare, he'd drop his gaze, or turn his head. And then a moment later, his eyes would find her again. The sadness there tugged on her heart.

Should it matter?

No. Never.

But it did.

This man had imprisoned her. He'd dragged her halfway across Europe, forcing her to face a madman.

True, that madman had been her brother and Mute had been as unaware of that as much as she.

"Mute?" She waited for a reply, but he only stared at her. Her voice was far more controlled than her pounding heart. "What is your favorite color?"

He blinked.

Twice.

Amazingly, a rumble began, morphing into a word. "Amber." He swallowed. "The color of your eyes."

Lia gasped. Something jerked on her heart, and she had to take several calming breaths to get it back to normal. When she was able to, she asked a simple question. "What time of the year? I mean, what season is your favorite?"

Mute was silent for so long she feared he wasn't going to answer.

Finally, he spoke. "Winter."

"Why?"

"It's never mattered one way or the other before, but I think it would be wonderful to be snowed in somewhere with... I mean it would be nice if there was nothing to do except snuggle in with someone for the duration of a winter storm."

"So, winter is a new favorite?"

"Yeah. Yes, it is."

"What was your old favorite?"

Mute lifted closed eyes to the ceiling and emitted a soft groan before admitting, "I didn't have a favorite season before."

"Before what?"

His dark eyes cut to hers. "Before you."

Lia couldn't speak.

The click-clacking of the train filled the silence. Three seconds passed. Five seconds.

Lia unfolded her arms, letting her fingers toy with the bottom of her shirt. "What's your favorite dessert?"

His voice was soft, almost inaudible. "What are you doing? Why the twenty questions?" He thrust out a hand, an obvious attempt at personal contact. But something held him back. At the last second, he lowered it.

Lia wondered why he didn't touch her.

And then why she didn't reach for that touch.

She searched his soul through those dark eyes. "I know nothing about you. How can I…" Lia clamped her mouth shut, stopping before she revealed too much. "There is so much I don't know about you." All she knew was he'd been born in Detroit, grew up on the streets, and became a Ranger before his present occupation.

A mercenary. A kidnapping mercenary.

Suddenly the truth hit her square in the forehead, and then in her heart. She'd already fallen for this man. Although his loyalties had previously been questionable, she loved this scarred, determined, honorable man. And whether he knew it or not, he had feelings for her.

So what? Even if their feelings were real, and not an infatuation due to raging adrenaline-filled hormones, where would that take them? Fairy tale endings were improbable in her world, impossible in his, so how could this work into a relationship?

She closed her eyes for a moment, trying to clear her head and stay on task. "I need to know more about you."

"Ask anything. Anything, at all. I'm an open book." His tone professed absolute truth. "You can ask me anything."

Lia inhaled deeply. Did she really want to know the answers? Yes.

No.

Yes.

Her voice was far too distrusting, even for her own ears. "Why didn't you leave after delivering me to Stepan? You had the opportunity. Stepan made sure of that." A hot, prickly sensation blurred her vision, and she had to blink rapidly to clear it. "You had the money in hand. You could have just left."

Mute reached for her hand, tucking it into his large one, and squeezed gently, before cradling both of their hands within his other. Finally, he looked up at her, his eyes teemed with guilt, but a glimmer of something else mutated the remorse into something far more powerful.

It took Lia several long moments to realize what it was.

Oh, My.

Never would she have believed it possible. This man didn't feel. Couldn't feel emotion. He couldn't.

Could he?

But there it was in his eyes.

Her heart caught.

Mute dropped his penetrating gaze, his attention focusing on their joined hands. "I couldn't leave you." A long sigh escaped him. "I could no more leave you in the hands of that..." Obviously giving up the search for the right word, he continued, "I couldn't leave you. No matter what."

For the first time in what seemed forever, the smile lifting her lips shone in her watering eyes.

But then, both the smile and the light created by it vanished as memories swamped her, memories of being bound and manhandled, of being forced to endure danger, robbed of freedom and even more importantly, her independence. "It's hard for me to wrap my tiny brain around what you are suggesting." Steel edged her tone. "It's far easier for me to equate you with my kidnapper..." Pain, as if a knife speared her heart, filled her when Mute cringed, but she managed to continue. "Than my savior."

Tense shoulders fell as his head dropped. A silent minute passed, feeling like an eternity.

Suddenly Mute smiled, his eyes meeting hers. Admittedly, it was timid and seemed completely out of character. But it was genuine. "I'm not the savior here, Lia." His grin widened a bit. "You are."

Lia jumped in her seat. She could feel heat flooding her cheeks. Her mouth rounded, but she couldn't speak.

Mute's shoulders relaxed and his grin took on epic proportions. "I can't believe how wrong I was, or how arrogant, when I spouted on and on about how I was born to save you. How my upbringing hardened me into the man to save you from your brother..." He glanced heavenward before dropping his gaze to the floor. Reaching for both her hands, clasping them within his warm grip, he added, "I was such an idiot."

Lia couldn't move. Shock paralyzed her. But it didn't matter.

"You saved me, Lia." Tenderness filled his eyes and his touch. "You saved me," he repeated. "I was so lost, so dead. I was only a shell that barely breathed."

The sadness filling his eyes was Lia's undoing. Tears shimmered in her eyes, spilling down smooth cheeks. "Oh, Mute…"

He placed a gentle finger against her open lips, effectively silencing her. "No. Let me finish." After sucking in a great breath, the kind so big it lifted those broad shoulders to head-level, he continued, "You showed me what living actually means. Your warmth, your zest…" he smiled. "Your indignation and determination against impossible odds. Damn, Lia." It took a moment before he could finish. "I wanted what you had. I wanted your passion. Your drive."

Mute's eyes darkened to pitch black. "And then I only wanted you."

After she gulped in a huge breath, Lia swiped away the tears coursing down her cheeks. "It doesn't matter…" she began.

Mute interrupted, pulling her into his side. "Yes, it does. It matters."

Her rolling eyes must have tipped him off, or the fact she pulled out of his arms.

Mute sighed as deep as those large lungs could without too much pain. "You can't begin to fathom my soulless life. It wasn't until you that I even understood how lifeless. There was nothing between one breath to the next." Somehow his husky voice deepened. "Until you."

"I will repeat this only once more." Her eyes narrowed. "It doesn't matter."

His head jerked back as if she'd slapped him.

Her tone softened. "I want two weeks."

Mute frowned, repeating, "Two weeks?"

Lia nodded.

"Two weeks for what?"

She sighed and lowered her gaze. "Two weeks without you."

A tic started in Mute's jaw. Finally, he asked, "Why?"

Glancing into his stricken face pained Lia and she had to turn away. Staring out the window, nothing registered. She only saw Mute's blurred reflection on the glass. Her chest tightened. Why did it seem there was no outside world when she was with him?

Lia straightened her spine. Lifting her head, she stared into his dark eyes. "I need to know if this is a Stockholm syndrome thing. Or if what I feel for you is real."

His sigh of relief was audible. Visibly relaxing, Mute's worried expression transformed into elation as he started to move, his intention to hold her clearly apparent.

Holding up a hand to stop him, she added, "I need separation, and that includes touching."

"Understood." Warmth filled his eyes, so much so, Lia wondered how in the world she'd once thought this man incapable of feeling.

She cleared her throat. "I'm going home. To my parents, to my way of life. I want my normal. I need to see if this…" she wagged a finger between their bodies. "Is something based on life-threatening situations or…" Her throat clogged again and for the life of her, she couldn't continue.

Mute picked up the slack. "Whatever you want, Lia. Take all the time you need." His voice dropped to a whisper. "I want you to want me as much as I want you."

Lia's chin tilted up. Her left eyebrow cocked. "Is it so hard to say the word 'love'?" Everything in her body stiffened, waiting. "Do you love me, Mute?"

The warmth in his eyes deepened, even as his pupils dilated. His lips lifted slightly at the corners before they dropped, and then the light in his face dimmed. Dropping his gaze, he finally answered, "I don't know what love is. It's not something I've ever known. Or even known existed."

Lia reached out, and using two fingers, lifted his chin so she could peer into his eyes. Everything she wanted to know lay stark naked in them. Her heart filled, swelling, but it wasn't enough. She needed him to recognize what he felt. "Mute? What do you think this is between us? What do you feel?"

Emotions raced across his face, each vying for dominance. Panic, then confusion, reflection, tenderness and finally, adoration. "I...I don't think there are words to describe what you make me feel. I'm not good at words anyway." He shoved his hands into the pockets of his pants, halting his reflexive reaching for her. "All I know, Lia, is I can't live without you." A deep sigh spilled from frowning lips. "I know what it is like. I've lived like the dead walking all my life. But, after meeting you, knowing you, wanting you, I couldn't go back to that kind of existence." Desperation filled his face and his voice. "I can't."

Lia knew her eyes were glistening with moisture, and she lowered her head so Mute wouldn't see. Blinking rapidly, she refused to give in to the tears. Her heart swelled again and she thought it might grow so big it would burst out of her chest. She forced her body to take slow, even breaths until her heart calmed. There was too much at stake for her to give in now. She still had so much to learn about this man.

She took another deep breath and then lifted her head, allowing a small smile to settle on her face. "What is your favorite movie?"

For a long time, he stared at her, and then a slow grin lifted the corners of his mouth. "I have more than one."

Her smile widened.

Mute's did too.

Ignoring her own directive, she reached for his hand, watching as she slowly entangled his fingers within her own. "Tell me about them all."

Twenty-Five

Mute had watched Lia enveloped within loving parental arms at the airport and then whisked away. She didn't even say goodbye, only gave him a quick glance over her shoulder as she was willingly dragged away.

He'd decided to stick around town. Two weeks weren't forever.

It had just seemed like it.

And then two weeks turned into three.

And then into four.

And then four weeks and two days.

Lia had finally contacted him, asking him to meet her. She had chosen this, a public venue.

The fact she'd texted instead of called was a bad sign. So was this place, a coffee shop teeming with people.

Worse was the fact it had been thirty-four days, eight hours, and twenty-nine minutes since he'd last had any physical contact with her.

He'd woken up on day fourteen with a smile on his face. The day had ended without any word from Lia. He thought he was going to go crazy.

The next day he knew he'd end up losing his mind if she didn't call soon.

A part of him died every day after that.

He'd wrestled with the decision to leave, to get on with his life. But what did it matter? Without Lia, he didn't have a life.

And now, he sat here in the last corner booth, watching the door, wondering if she would show. He glanced at his watch. Seventeen minutes passed ten. She'd said ten. He'd arrived fifteen minutes early. He'd been here over half an hour.

Mute sighed, knowing his butt was glued to this seat until Lia showed up, it didn't matter if that was a minute or a year from now. Lava Java was his new address.

The bell on the door rang, signaling its opening or closing. Mute's head popped up and then down. Someone left. He glanced at his watch again. Eighteen minutes after ten. His head rose, and he gazed out the expansive window, at the people passing in front of the coffee shop.

People scurried to and fro, an endless sea of color. Most had their heads down as if looking at their feet or their phones.

Something grabbed his attention. That woman held her head up, her stride purposeful.

His heart caught. He knew that profile, that gorgeous face.

Mute leaped up, his hip catching the corner of the table, upsetting it. The two cups of coffee sitting there flew through the air.

The bell on the door sounded.

A male voice at the next table yelled, "Hey!"

Mute stood in the aisle, his stare centered on Lia as she entered the room.

A man stood, coffee dripping from his shirt and down his pants. "What the…" He glowered at Mute. "Look, buddy, an apology isn't going to cut…"

Mute couldn't breathe. His heart stopped. Lia wasn't smiling. A hole burned through his stomach. He took a step toward her.

A hand clamped onto his bicep, halting his forward momentum. Mute's focus remained on Lia. Her eyes were searching the room until they latched onto his. She stopped, hesitated for a moment, before striding in his direction.

Taking a step, needing to reach her, to touch her, to hold her---Mute was surprised to find himself held in place.

The hand trying to keep him from Lia had to go.

"Look, man, you need to pay for..."

Without breaking their locked gazes, Mute reached out and plucked the hand from his arm, mumbling, "Later." He took another step toward Lia.

Resolution and a healthy dose of anxiety filled her expression.

Mute breathed out her name. "Lia?"

She reached for his hand, intertwining their fingers, and stared down at them. Her head remained downcast for several seconds.

Mute froze. He didn't know if he could take the rejection coming.

Yes, he did.

He couldn't.

His throat clogged, strangling his voice. "Lia?"

Lia raised her head. Tears glistened on her eyelashes like diamonds, her amber eyes shining like bright gold in the sunshine as her gaze traveled over his face. A sob caught in her throat and her free hand flew up, landing at the base of her throat.

And then she lifted their tangled hands and kissed the back of his. Amber eyes, full of compassion, so full of love, gazed up at him from beneath long, dark eyelashes.

Breath filled his lungs and Mute inhaled deeply, the overpowering aroma of cream and coffee almost masking Lia's sweet scent. His heart skipped a beat and a half and then revved into a speed rivaling Nascar. For a long moment, he couldn't find his voice, but somehow, he managed to rumble, "Lia."

Everything he was feeling---elation, awe, humbleness, but most of all, love poured into her name. He reached for her and enveloped her within his arms, cradling her soft body against his. It wasn't until she wrapped one leg around his calves he realized he'd picked her up.

"I love you, Mute. I didn't want to. I tried not to. But…" She stared at him with so much warmth his heart melted. Her voice trailed to a whisper. "I love you."

He set her down so he could cradle her beautiful face in his hands. Her name was a prayer from his lips. "Lia." He searched her face, every line, every curve, God, he loved that little mole above her lips. Still, it was the love shining from her eyes convincing him. He breathed her name again, his heart in every syllable. "Lia."

A laugh sounded behind him. "Sheesh, dude. Is that all you can say?" A powerful hand clamped onto Mute's shoulder. "Look, Romeo, you're supposed to say you love her too, the sun rises and sets with her, that she's your everything, and, oh yeah, you can't live without her."

A tear slipped down Lia's cheek, but she never took her eyes off his. Her voice was assured, despite the softness of her whisper. "He did." The beginnings of a smile hovered at her lips. "He said all that and more."

And then she jumped into his arms, wrapping her body around his and kissed him.

Like there was no tomorrow.

The room erupted with shouts and clapping from a coffee shop full of captivated on-lookers.

~*~

With one exception.

At the opposite end of the room, a sleek, serpentine woman tapped her nails to the beat of a silent rhythm. Or rather, it was more of a tap, tap, click, click. The sound repeated. Tap, tap, click, click. The woman, dressed in black silk, didn't clap, only continued tapping her nails on the table.

A sunbeam hit her hand, and gold flashed in its light to each click, click. The long nails tapped one more time and then her sharpened talons slowly etched a long, deep scratch into the wooden table top.

And then another.

A perfect X.

Please visit your favorite book-site and leave a review. Reviews are always wanted and greatly appreciated. It is through reviews, like yours, authors generate interest and gain new readers. It also helps readers, like you, find new books you'll love to read over and over. Thank you.

About the Author

Dancing to a slightly different drummer has been more of an advantage than a handicap for Crysa James. It has enabled her to pen stories in many different genres of fiction, including science fiction, suspense, horror, mystery, western, inspirational, and children's literature.

Her first love will always be Romance, any kind of Romance, running the gambit from historical to Contemporary and most everything in between.

Her East Texas hearth and home are full, with her very own hero husband, two wonderful children, and a menagerie of best friends from the animal kingdom.

Please enjoy an excerpt from Crysa James's upcoming novel.

Mourning Rose

Chapter One

"Dammit, John, I don't have time to babysit."
Rock Stevenson glared at his partner of almost two
decades. "And... and… this is no place for a woman.
I don't care if her last name is the same as the
President's." His furious scowl thinned sculpted lips.
"What's her name again? Jan? Joan?"

The pair had started *High Country Outrider*,
the premier hunting service in central Colorado, over
eighteen years ago. They provided professionally
guided trips into what only the Rockies could
provide---world class trophy hunts among rugged,
wild and sometimes treacherous beauty. Or if John
had his way at the moment, a photo excursion. Rock
shook his head, silently shouting his opinion about
this ludicrous idea.

"Jenna. Jenna Faulkner." John answered
automatically. "She needs a guide who can show her
the best places to take pictures." His hand rose, palm
open, as if the gesture could calm a furious Rock.
"Apparently, the necessity is real for Mrs. Faulkner is
adamant about the *now*." His voice remained calm
and low.

His partner, not so much. "Don't care. Don't
care *why*. Don't *want* to know." Rock punched the air
with his forefinger, hitting an imaginary spot just
under John's nose, his voice thunderous. "It's too
early in the season. You know as well as I do bears
aren't even starting to hibernate." Although it seemed
deliberate, his pause was anything but. "Hell, John,

we haven't even had our first snow." Unconsciously, Rock lifted his cowboy hat and wiped the sweat off his brow with a sweep of his forearm.

"Mrs. Faulkner has been informed of the dangers. She's determined the…" John paused, obviously searching for the right word for this endeavor had nothing to do with hunting. "Trip starts now." John's eyes filled with concern and his voice softened. "I have a feeling she can't wait." Locking troubled eyes with Rock's angry ones, he continued, "Look. I didn't deliberately mislead you. And I'm sorry you're stuck with this. It was always my intention to guide for Mrs. Faulkner, but this damn busted leg won't let me." John impatiently tapped the brand-new cast covering his left leg. "I knew you wouldn't want to do it. Nevertheless, I'd already accepted full payment and I couldn't very well say at the last minute 'Here's your money back. Sorry you traveled all this way for nothing', now could I?"

Rock dug the toe of his well-worn cowboy boot into the dirt. Dust hung, low in the dry air around the indention. A grating noise broke the awkward silence. Rock's nasty habit of grinding his teeth when upset returned with a vengeance. "Yeah. You could." He straightened his already rigid back, glowering at his partner.

John finally answered, low and insistent, "No. I couldn't."

Rock remained still, studying his friend. Suddenly his shoulders slumped and he expelled a long-held breath. Dropping his stare, he grudgingly agreed, "Yeah, okay, I guess you couldn't." Anger again surged, deepening his already dark brown eyes.

"Why does she insist on going now? What's the advantage? This country hasn't changed for thousands, hell, hundreds of thousands of years. Why can't she wait a couple, three months?" His gaze sidled away, as he ignored the usual cacophony blaring this time of year at HCO headquarters.

Trying to curb his temper, Rock sought solace in the vast landscape of snowcapped mountains. Not surprising, he made out a small herd of mule deer enjoying breakfast on a far slope. Still, try as he might, nothing seemed to tame the simmering resentment. Dark eyes again bore into his life-long friend.

"Mrs. Faulkner has expressed the need to pack into the high country for a week. She intends to shoot nothing more than pictures. A slight frown lowered set lips. "Although nothing's been mentioned, she seems, well, um, she insists the trip can't be postponed." Apology tinged his tone. "As in after I'm healed and can ride again." Regret filled John's eyes. "I'm sorry, Rock. I fully intended to do the honors myself. I know you don't like to mollycoddle our guests and ninety percent don't need it. You know I'm always happy to handle the ones that do." His tone lightened slightly. "However, Mrs. Faulkner swears she's physically up to the challenge."

Rock snorted. "Yeah. Right. Sure she is. Like any woman knows how tough you've got to be. Both mentally and physically." Giving his partner an incredulous glare, he continued. "Hell, John, few men do." Expressive brows knotted furiously, his posture stiff and unyielding. "You know as well as I do, most hunters arrive thinking they are in excellent shape.

They learn quick they should have done a hell of a lot more conditioning. Few are physically fit enough." He couldn't help repeating, "And you know it."

John unconsciously nodded. "Can't argue with you, but it really shouldn't be a problem anyway. The lady is only taking pictures. There's no need to stalk up or down a mountain, searching for a trophy bull elk, or trying to spot a monster buck. You will be the only one with a gun. Her weapon of choice is a Canon, I think."

"What about Clint?" Rock's gaze went skyward as he considered alternatives. "Or Jared?" One arm swept wildly, cutting the air. "Hell, even Aaron can take her…"

John shook his head, cutting Rock off. "Think about it. The woman has paid, in full, the entire fee for a full hunt. That's a week under the stars for a group of, at minimum, five." A deep frown settled on his face. "A woman who can afford that kind of fee won't hesitate to sue if one of our employees so much as makes a pass at her. We can't afford a lawsuit, Rock." John drew in a quick breath, pinning Rock with a knowing look. "Talk about a nightmare."

"Okay. Well, then. I guess Clint's out." Both knew Clint chased anything remotely resembling a skirt. "But not Jared. And Aaron's just out of diapers."

John interrupted. "Are you willing to bet High Country Outriders on that?"

Rock pondered a long moment before shaking his head. *Of course not.* "Look." Rock finally spoke, "Why can't we send out a third man with Jared and this client? Better yet, Aaron. He's just a kid and doesn't have the guts to make a pass at an older woman." His features screwed up. "She *is* a mature woman, isn't she?

"Yes. Her application said mid-forties. I'd have to review her file to be more accurate." John's frown deepened. "But it doesn't matter, Rock. Jared's not due until next month. Same thing with Aaron. And before you even ask, Wash and W.T. are tied up scouting."

Rock hated the sympathy on John's face. He hated the truth of the matter even more. His teeth ground together, clipping the snarl surfacing. Instead, he threaded pure disgust into his statement. "This is foolhardy. A waste of time. Absolutely ludicrous. She's gonna gripe and moan every step we take. And you want me to put up with this for a full week?" He didn't give John time to answer. "So what if she wants to take a few pictures. Hand her a dozen postcards and call it done, John." Rock's statement asked the question and they both knew it.

"I can't."

"Why not?"

"She's already here."

Every cell in Rock's body was paralyzed for a long moment as the words registered. And then his volcanic temper erupted. One powerful fist swung up, hitting the palm of his opposite and equally powerful hand. Although the gesture wasn't pleasant, it wasn't from the resultant pain that Rock roared. "Ah shit, John. Where? How did…" A small measure of disappointment crept into his furious eyes. "When were you going to tell me?"

"I just did." John stood still, regret etched on his face.

Rock cursed under his breath. Suddenly a violent gush of breath exploded from his tight lips. "Well, she's going to have to find a motel for tonight 'cause, uh, I'm not ready. It's gonna take the rest of the day to load up and pack."

John's shoulders relaxed the slightest bit. Holding onto a slight grimace, John nodded before placing a comforting hand on Rock's broad shoulder and then squeezing. "Yes, you are. The horses are already packed and waiting. Giselle has been saddled for Mrs. Faulkner. Your horse is ready, too. All you need is to throw a few duds in your saddlebags."

Rock's mouth opened, understanding hitting as hard as a ton of bricks. *I just agreed to this... this... of all the dumb, stupid...* Cringing with every part of his body, including his face, it was hard to speak for a moment.

But speak he finally did. And loudly. "I see. Any more surprises? Is there anything else you're waiting for the *right time* to tell me?"

John only shook his head. The fine lines around his mouth and eyes, etched from decades outdoors, softened. "Nope. That's it, Rock.

"Mrs. Faulkner paid for a week-long trek in the mountains and that's what she's going to get. I hate the privilege is all yours since I'm laid up and unavailable." John's tone hardened. "But you are to show her the best of the back country in all its wondrous splendor and see that while she rests in the bosom of God, nothing, and I mean nothing, harms our paying guest in any way, shape, form, or fashion."

Rock stood still. The fury swelling within turned his eyes cold.

John waited expectantly.

Rock's mouth tightened into a flat, straight line. Giving his partner his best glare, he started to speak. His mouth opened, and then closed.

John obviously knew better than to interfere with Rock's inner war. And as usual, his delay met with satisfactory results.

Finally, Rock's dark eyes conceded defeat. "Okay." Throwing his hands wide, he all but shouted, "All right John. I get it. A paying customer is a paying customer. Whether it's a hunting expedition or picture taking. I get it." Abruptly his eyes narrowed and his voice hardened. "And when money changes hands, it doesn't matter if those hands are female or male. Or whether he or she is capable or not. Our job is to please the customer." Rock's gaze leveled directly into his partner's. "Can't say I'm good at that crap of *the customer is always right*, for you know as well as anyone in our line of work, that shit gets people killed." Rock leveled a drill of a finger at John's nose. "And that someone could be them. Or me."

The sound of crunching rocks and gravel split the tension hanging in the air as the men faced each other. An ancient but serviceable station wagon crept up the driveway toward the main entrance of HCO.

Although highly questionable as to fine or foul, Mrs. Jenna Faulkner had arrived.

Rock Stevenson, of High Country Outriders, would just have to deal with it.

Chapter Two

Jenna Faulkner waited until the taxi came to a complete stop before she emerged from the vehicle. Taking a quick, but thorough, survey of the immediate area, she had to admit the scenery was in keeping with her expectations of what a hunting lodge located deep in the Rocky Mountains would look like. Reddish brown log cabins, compact and square, dotted the edges of the gravel drive leading to a stately but epic Log House. Three stories tall, it dwarfed everything around it except for the spindly trees shading the cabins. White pines, she guessed. Blue columbine and bold zinnias graced the landscaping around each cabin, adding wondrous color in an already gorgeous vista. Horses grazed in pastures adjacent to a huge two-story barn, adding their own special color and tranquility to the picturesque scene.

What she hadn't expected were the two hard-bitten cowboys embroiled in a stand-off outside the main building. It wasn't hard to recognize the battle going on before her. No matter. Not her ballgame. Whatever their problem, it didn't involve her.

Ignoring the tension, she strode to the closest cowboy--the tall one in blue jeans and black leather chaps.

In the time it took to cross the barren yard, Jenna studied his harsh, strong features. That square, stubborn chin. The long, straight nose. Glaring dark cocoa eyes. The vehemence in his gaze surprised her.

Normally, the exorbitant fees she'd already paid insured genuine hospitality.

A frown formed on her lips and a sinking feeling hit the bottom of her stomach. *This isn't going to be good.*

The shorter man immediately limped toward her, his grin wide. His open hand reached for hers, swallowing it, pumping enthusiastically. An odd sense of relief helped her tight stomach.

"Welcome, Mrs. Faulkner. I'm John Milton, co-owner and founder of High Country Outriders. We look forward to serving you." John's welcoming smile deepened.

Jenna smiled back. "Thank you, Mr. Milton. It's a pleasure to finally meet you. I'm looking forward to this little adventure."

The other man's derisive snort startled her and her emerald eyes cut sharply in his direction.

John Milton introduced his partner. "And this…" one quick jerk of a thumb indicated the angry cowboy, "Is your guide, Rock Stevenson." Smiling brightly, John offered, "Whatever you need, we will provide. All you have to do is ask."

One look at the tall, angry man next to John prompted her unusual and off-the-cuff remark. "Another guide, perhaps?"

Mourning Rose

By

Crysa James

Coming Soon

Crysa James loves hearing
from her readers.
Be sure to stop in and chat.
Anytime.

Website:
www.crysajames.com

Twitter:
www.twitter.com/CrysaJ

Facebook Page:
www.facebook.com/CrysaJames

www.ingramcontent.com/pod-product-compliance
Lightning Source LLC
Chambersburg PA
CBHW051944220626
47052CB00004B/793